Innocent In
Las Vegas

A. R. Winters

Innocent in Las Vegas
Copyright 2013 by A. R. Winters

This book is licensed for your personal enjoyment only.

***

Innocent In Las Vegas (A Tiffany Black Story)

***

Private investigator by day, blackjack dealer by night, and cupcake-addict extraordinaire, Tiffany Black has just landed her first case. Casino owner Ethan Becker has been murdered, and Tiffany needs to find the real killer.

What should have been a simple matter of talking to a few suspects gets out of hand, and soon Tiffany finds herself fielding violent casino goons, a mysterious new bodyguard and strange masked men. Her poker-playing Nanna and pushy parents want Tiffany to settle down and get a nice husband, but Tiffany just wants to stay alive and solve the case, preferably with a few more cupcakes for good luck...

CHAPTER ONE

Despite the bags under her eyes and the ankle monitor, Sophia Becker looked gorgeous.

"Tiffany!" She flashed a phony smile and embraced me in a warm hug. Her voice contained trace amounts of anxiety and relief, and her beautiful blue eyes couldn't hide her worry. "I'm so glad you came!"

I shrugged nonchalantly. I didn't want her to get her hopes up, or to think our relationship had changed. "I was told it wouldn't hurt to listen."

"Well, thank you for coming."

I walked behind her, my low-heeled sandals making a clicking noise against the white marble floor. Her place smelled expensive, like a Vanilla-Bergamot scented candle, and was so clean and tidy that I wondered just how many staff she employed.

When we reached the far side of the living room, Sophia slid gracefully into a wooden chair, and crossed her long, tan legs. She was wearing a short black miniskirt and a designer tank top, and her ankle monitor flashed silently. "Richard's filled you in?"

"He told me you're looking for a PI, but didn't give me details." I perched gingerly on an antique armchair worth more than my entire month's salary. In my casual Bermuda shorts and t-shirt, I felt a little out of place in this glamorous room. "Although, I don't really see what a PI can do for you at this stage."

Sophia flipped her long blonde hair from one side of her face to the other, and her elegant diamond drop earrings shimmered in the light. She gave me a pained look. "I'm innocent. Don't you believe that?"

"That's what they all say. And even if you are, it's hard to argue against the evidence."

"It was planted."

I sighed. "Sophia, they found the gun in your nightstand. Literally. A. Smoking. Gun."

She stared at me for a second, an angry fire dancing in her eyes, and then she leaned back in her chair and visibly relaxed. "Do you think I'm stupid?"

I shook my head. I didn't even have to think about that one. She was anything but stupid.

Sophia was beautiful, friendly and witty – and she put those qualities to good use by becoming a stripper. She was also ruthless and ambitious, and that was probably how she managed to make Ethan Becker, owner of the Riverbelle Casino, fall in love with her.

Thanks to Ethan's wealth, Sophia's stripping days had been put behind her as soon as they got engaged, and the wedding was exclusive and ostentatious. Judging from the massive rocks she wore, and the Lake Las Vegas mansion I was sitting in right now, Sophia's marital life had been one great big fairytale.

Until three months ago, when her husband was murdered.

"Then why," she said, "Does everyone think I'm dumb enough to wipe down a murder weapon and put it back in my nightstand?"

"Maybe you didn't think anyone would look?" Sophia narrowed her eyes and I went on, "Someone would have to break in to plant the gun in your bedroom. You never reported a break-in."

"I couldn't tell from the lock. There are good lock-pickers, you know."

I looked at her doubtfully. "And what do you want me to do?"

"Find out what the police overlooked."

"What makes you think they overlooked anything?"

"Oh, please. The instant they found that gun, they stopped all investigations and acted like I'd confessed to doing it. Meanwhile, the guy who killed my husband is walking free."

I took a moment to think about it. Did I really think Sophia had killed Ethan? It was hard to tell – all through our high-school years she'd been a good actress, manipulating people to get her way. She'd been the pretty, popular cheerleader who'd spread mean rumors behind your back and then teased you about your weight, your hair and your unfashionable clothes. I hadn't been too fond of her back then, and I wasn't sure what she was capable of now.

As though she'd read my mind, Sophia said, "Why would I kill my husband? I had a great life, and I'd be stupid to risk all that."

"I don't know. What if I find things that incriminate you further? You know I'll have to tell the cops."

Sophia nodded. "Of course."

I thought about all the reasons I didn't want to take on this case. "Why me? Why not someone else?"

"It's a great first case."

I loved the way she didn't answer me directly. I wasn't even fully accredited, and she wanted me to look into something so serious. "How'd you find me anyway?"

"Ed Hastings recommended you."

Ed was my supervising detective. He certified to the Nevada Board of Private Investigators that I wasn't mentally unstable or criminally inclined, and once a month I did ten hours of supervised work for him – mostly boring surveillance details. My one year of supervised work was almost up, and I was grateful to Ed for the recommendation, even if I wasn't too keen on the client.

"Richard Small did a background check," Sophia continued, "And then he contacted you."

I tried my best not to smirk. Richard might be a successful defense attorney, but I wondered how he'd gotten through high school with such an unfortunate name. He'd probably survived his name the same way I'd survived mine.

My mother, in her infinite love of all things sparkly and shiny, had named me Tiffany. Tiffany Black. Almost every day of my short 28-year-old life I'd heard someone, usually a rat-eyed creep with bad breath, coo out a variation of the romantic phrase, "You have a stripper name, you must really like poles."

Having a stripper name meant that I went out of my way to not look like a stripper. That involved having unruly brown hair which refused to be tamed, carrying a protective layer of cushioning fat around my waistline, and wearing more clothes than all the local Vegas girls combined.

I said, "No-one else will take the work, will they?"

Sophia glanced away and I smiled triumphantly. Of course she wouldn't voluntarily want to employ a no-name, not-quite-accredited PI like myself if she had better options. She'd hired one of the best defense attorneys in the state, and she could afford any PI – if they'd just agree to work for her.

"It's really simple work–" she began, but I interrupted her.

"No, it's not, and you know it. No-one messes with the casino owners."

"I *am* a casino owner," she said. "At least I will be, if you can help me get off. Then you'll have an easy time getting jobs."

"*If.* And that's a big if."

We looked at each other silently. Jobs here were dependent on the casinos, and nobody wanted to get on the wrong side of the powerful few who controlled an entire state's economy.

"Please, Tiff." Sophia looked at me with sad eyes. "I need you to help me out. I'm in a terrible place, and if you won't help, I don't know what to do."

Her eyes brimmed with tears and I looked away. *Crap.* I felt like I was kicking a puppy. Despite whatever she'd done when we were younger, the woman was living a nightmare now, and I wouldn't wish that on anyone.

I glanced at my watch and stood up quickly. "I should go. I'm late."

Sophia sniffed. "Please, tell me you'll at least consider this?"

I looked at her carefully. She'd always been an expert manipulator and I hated the thought of being pushed into doing something I didn't want to. But her face was pinched, and I could almost smell the doom surrounding her.

"I'll think about it," I said, "It could be a great opportunity for someone." *To shoot themselves in the foot.*

Sophia nodded, and showed me out silently.

CHAPTER TWO

Vegas drivers are the worst in the world. Not me, of course. But everyone else.

As I drove east along the Las Vegas Beltway, I had to stifle my urge to make rude hand gestures and lean on the horn. I hadn't been lying about being late, and I was grateful Sophia hadn't asked what I was late for. She probably already knew.

I stopped at my condo, a tiny, one-bedroom place I'd managed to buy right after the market crashed, and changed. I could drive to work, but the best thing about my place is that it's only a three-block walk into work.

The Strip is a nightmare to drive down at night – all it takes is one mesmerized tourist staring at the lights to cause a pileup. The late evening breeze made it cool enough to walk, even in the middle of the scorching summer, and I told myself I was getting some much-needed exercise.

As soon as I entered the casino pit, the loudness hit me: all the colors, noises and lights that epitomized Sin City. Walking into the madness felt like meeting an old friend – a boisterous old friend who annoys you at first, but grows on you.

I tapped out the day-shift dealer, clapped my hands to show that they were empty, and smiled around the table. "Are you guys having a good time?"

I genuinely cared about how the men felt. My tips depended upon it. Two of them smiled in a vague, non-committal way, but one took my question seriously.

"Fucking blackjack," he said. "The other fucking dealer was screwing me over. I hope you're here to improve my fucking luck."

He looked at me suspiciously, as though I might have a secret nefarious motive for being there. I smiled and motioned the waitress. "Looks like you need a refill on that drink."

He grunted distrustfully and I started dealing. I knew the man well. He was one of the regulars at any table, Mr. Here For The Fucking Money. His real name varied but he was always the same person – rude, surly and generous with the F-bombs. Inevitably he always lost and it was always the 'fucking casino's fault', which meant 'no fucking tip for the dealer'.

At least none of my other regulars were there: Mr. Body Odor, Mr. Perving On Every Woman Around, and Mr. Cigar Man.

I focused on the cards and pretty soon Mr. Here For The Fucking Money busted out, threw a hissy fit, and left the table to do God-knows-what. His place was quickly taken by three frat boys, who all thought they were giving Don Juan a run for his money: "Whatchya doing after work?", "You wanna show us around Vegas?" (wink wink) and of course, "Met a stripper named Tiffany yesterday, that wasn't you, was it?"

I tell myself every day that I don't hate my job. It doesn't pay as much as stripping or being a cocktail waitress, but I get to wear more clothes, don't get perved on as much, and never get groped. But there's a reason I'm trying to leave the madness of the casino pit to become a Private Investigator, and it was a relief when I got a tap on my shoulder, indicating that it was time for my break.

I headed into the break room and checked my voicemail. There was a strange message from my grandmother, and I told myself I'd call her back tomorrow. I was expecting Sophia to have left me a message reminding me to think about things, but she was clearly giving me some space.

I felt like I was being chicken, that if I were braver I would just jump straight into the work. But that would be foolhardy – no other PI would touch the case for a reason: clearly there was no chance of wrapping it up successfully. A failed, high-profile case would be damaging for any established PI's reputation and fatal for any newbie's career.

I didn't like Sophia much but she was convincing in her declarations of innocence. Part of the reason I'd chosen to try to be a PI was so I could help people, and Sophia was desperately in need of help. Plus, I knew she'd be willing to pay me an exorbitant amount of money to do the investigating.

All through the night I watched people wager on games biased in the house's favor. And yet, players frequently walked away with much more than they lost. The Vegas adage, "You gotta play to win," was true.

By the time my shift ended, I'd managed to convince myself that I needed to take on Sophia's case. It was a gamble that had the potential to pay off well, so I sent Sophia a quick text.

If I had known then that I would be risking my life for the case, I would have talked myself out of taking it. In retrospect, I wonder why I didn't realize that a person who had already committed one murder would stop at nothing to prevent further damning evidence from being unearthed.

CHAPTER THREE

The next morning I found myself back at Sophia's mansion. She looked pleased to see me; there was a hopefulness in her eyes that was heartbreaking and made me want to drop the case just so I wouldn't have to disappoint her.

But I didn't. Instead, I handed her a standard retainer agreement and watched her initial it and sign on the dotted line. As soon as she'd finished with the contract, Sophia brought out some tea for herself and some chocolate cupcakes for me. For a few long minutes, all I could think about was how chocolate cupcakes make life so much better.

I paused my cupcake-demolishing long enough to say, "What do I need to know? Who do I talk to?"

Sophia sipped her tea gracefully. "Neil Durant. My brother-in-law. He was the chief suspect before they found that gun; he's probably the one who killed Ethan."

I recalled what I'd learned in my pre-meeting online research. Ethan Becker had been driving home on a Saturday night at around 1 a.m. and had pulled over to the side of the road. At that hour, on a deserted suburban street, nobody was around. Someone had shot him and the crime was only discovered by an early-morning jogger at 5 a.m.

"Whaffuzzushayet?" I asked.

Sophia gave me a funny look and I swallowed quickly. "What makes you say that?"

"Night of the murder, Ethan and Neil went to a dinner near The Strip. Neil lives nearby and he would've taken the same route home. But even though he and Ethan left at the same time, Neil got home two hours later and has no alibi for those two hours. He says he took a windy road home – yeah, right!"

I stopped my feral gobbling for a moment. "So what you're saying is, Neil should've discovered the car and called the police?"

"Doesn't that make sense? He claims he took a round-about by-road, but why would you do that when you're going home, tired after a dinner?"

"That's a little suspicious, but it's not really proof."

"His wife Thelma – Ethan's sister – claims Neil got home at three and they spent the rest of the night together."

"But why would he kill Ethan? Did they have a problem or something?"

Sophia looked at the floor. For the first time, I noticed the sadness in her eyes. "I'm not sure, but I know they argued a lot. A few days before the murder, they had a big fight about something. Ethan wasn't happy with some of Neil's ideas for the casino. I mean, it's not like Neil had any casino background or anything, he used to be an underwear model."

"You didn't do any work for the casino?"

"I didn't bother. Ethan, his sister Thelma, and Neil were all board members, but not me. People already thought I was a gold-digger."

"But weren't you?"

Sophia laughed, refusing to take offence. I'd only asked her what most people thought but never said aloud. "I was a stripper," she said, "And *Ethan Becker* asked me to marry him. How could I not say yes?"

I loved the way her mouth formed words but didn't really answer the question. "Did Ethan leave you much in the will?"

"It's split between me and his son, Leo. Of course, Thelma is going after me with a civil case. And if I lose that, Leo and Thelma divvy up my share."

"Who owns the casino?"

"After their dad passed away, Thelma got 40% of the casino shares and Ethan got 55%. The other 5% are owned by family friends and early investors. At this stage, Leo gets half of his dad's casino shares and some cash. I get the other half of Ethan's shares, and some other assets. If Thelma wins her case, Leo probably gets the casino shares I have, and Thelma gets the other assets Ethan left me."

"Thelma and Ethan – were they close?"

"I guess, in a way." Sophia shrugged. "She wasn't too fond of me, which I understand, but it still hurt and I was hoping we'd become friends. But now, none of the family will talk to me."

"And Leo? He's got motive, with all that inheritance money."

"Maybe my judgment's been compromised, but I don't think Leo could do that to his dad. I just can't see him…" She shook her head. "Anyway, he has an excellent alibi. Night of the murder, he was partying till dawn with fifty of his friends."

"How old is Leo?"

"Twenty-one. He's a student at UNLV. Here." She handed me a piece of paper. "It's a list of names, relationships and contact details for everyone you should talk to."

I ran my eyes down the list. Thelma Durant, sister. Neil Durant, brother-in-law. Leo Becker, son. I paused. "Vanessa Conigliani, ex-wife?"

"Ethan's first wife. They split ten years ago. Leo's mom."

I nodded. "Is there anyone else I should talk to, other than family? Who else is on the casino board? This might be related to Ethan's work."

Sophia looked up a contact on her phone and wrote down a name. Steven Macarthur, Manager. "He's on the board," she said, "But he was on the casino floor the entire night, watching a group of blackjack players. He's recorded on camera for literally every second of that night. And besides, he and Ethan got on really well. Ethan adored him, thought he could do no wrong."

"Four people on the board?"

"The fifth was Laura Schumaker, but she's the corporate lawyer and isn't involved in the business."

"Anything else I should know?"

Sophia shook her head. "Not that I can think of. But I should tell you, Neil never liked me and we never got along. He was always saying unkind things about me behind my back, and I've always thought he's one of those good-looking bull-shitters that's faking their way into places."

It takes one to know one. I finished my cupcake slowly, savoring the rich chocolaty goodness, and wondered if Sophia was judging Neil too harshly through the lens of her own prejudice. I was sure his arriving home late on the night of the murder was just a coincidence, and I wondered where else I could begin my investigation.

CHAPTER FOUR

By the time I left Sophia's house, I'd decided to talk to Neil another day. I was going to talk to Leo Becker first. Motive-wise he had the most to gain and people had committed crimes for far less than the millions of dollars Ethan had left his son. Leo did have a great alibi, but still…

I glanced at the address Sophia had given me and headed west. I took the ramp onto the 515 and, after a few minutes of enduring crazy expressway drivers, I took the Flamingo exit. A few minutes later, I found myself at Swenson.

Leo's apartment was in a nondescript brown building, near the UNLV campus. I sat in my car for a few minutes, watching people coming and going. Most were in their twenties; it seemed like a popular place for students to rent. I gave myself a little pep talk as I sat by myself – I was going to be the tough investigator and I was going to get the information I needed out of this kid. He didn't stand a chance against me.

A few minutes later, I was standing near the building's gate, looking down at the list of names Sophia had given me, wondering if it would've been best to call ahead. Probably not.

A youngish-looking man walked out of the building, and held the security door open for me. "Are you visiting someone?"

He was annoyingly young and looked at me like I was someone's kindly aunt. I would've been happier if he'd realized that I have youthful good looks, but this was work, so I played along with the part, and said in an aunt-like voice, "Leo Becker. Do you know him?"

"Yeah, sure. Easy-going guy."

He smiled and left, and I made my way to Leo's apartment. I knocked twice and after a while the door was opened by a young man with disheveled hair and crumpled clothes.

"Leo Becker?"

He blinked slowly, stretched and looked at me in confusion. "Yeah?"

"Mind if I come in?" I held up my PI's badge. It didn't mean much, but Leo didn't know that.

He stumbled away from the door and I closed it behind myself.

"Just a second." Leo left me alone to go to the bathroom and I heard the sounds of splashing water.

I used the time as an opportunity to look around. There wasn't much to see – it was a tiny studio apartment, with a bed on one side of the room, a desk and three chairs, a flat-screen TV, and clothes on the floor. The kitchenette must have been added as an after-sight. It wasn't practical for anything other than heating up leftovers, though that was probably all it was ever used for. I imagined Leo cleaning up the place to have a girl visit, and I could see that happening. But I couldn't imagine him hosting a party, or having friends over to watch the Superbowl.

I hadn't expected such a normal place. I'd imagined Leo living in somewhere ostentatious, acting like the rich kid he was.

He emerged from the bathroom looking slightly more awake and stumbled over to the desk, where he sat down, closed his eyes and pressed his fingers against his eyelids. Ah, college hangovers. I noticed a Nespresso machine on the counter, and before I could help it, I said, "Would you like me to make you a coffee?"

I had actually turned into a kindly old aunt.

Thankfully, Leo shook his head and wandered over to the coffee machine himself. I couldn't help feeling relieved – I'm hopelessly incompetent when it comes to making things in the kitchen, even simple things like a cup of coffee. If Leo had left the coffee-making to me, I would probably have wound up breaking the machine, and flooding the tiny kitchenette floor with hot water and milk.

Leo went about inserting pods wordlessly and making his drink. There was something helpless and naïve about him that made me feel strangely empathetic. It was obvious why Sophia thought he could never be a killer.

As I watched him pour out the coffee, I said, "Big party last night?"

Leo nodded silently.

"Do you party much?"

"No."

Finally, a word! Though it was really more of a groan.

I waited quietly for a few minutes as Leo gulped down his coffee like it was some disgusting medicine. I didn't have high hopes about it helping with his hangover, but it might make him feel more awake, or at the very least, feel a bit more like talking.

When he finished his drink, he turned and faced me. "What's this about?"

"I'm looking into your father's murder. Do you think Sophia did it?"

Sadness washed over his face briefly, and I wondered how he was handling the death. Leo shook his head. "I never liked her, but I don't think she did it."

"Why didn't you like her?"

He shrugged. "She's too young. Dad can marry whoever he wants, but really? Marrying a stripper, at his age, how much more of a cliché can you be?"

"Did you see her much?"

"Hardly. We had a few dinners and she tried to be friendly, but who cares? I expected him to divorce her after a few years anyway, like he divorced my mom. I stayed out of her way."

"Right." I wanted to ask about Ethan's divorce, but I decided to wait. "So what makes you think she didn't do it?"

He looked at me for a long time and then finally said, "I forgot about the gun. So she did it, huh?"

"I don't know, I'm asking you what you think."

"She married him for the money. Why would she kill him?" There was a long pause and then he shrugged. "Maybe she found out about one of his girls. Maybe she really did love him."

I tried not to let my surprise show. "What girls?"

Leo looked at me, narrowed his eyes and laughed shortly. "Dad always has – had— girls. He was never faithful to my mom. I can't imagine he's changed."

"How do you know he wasn't faithful?"

"Mom told me, later on. And I could tell. He's no saint. You think he stopped seeing strippers just because he married one?"

It was my turn to stare at Leo. His words were giving me the creeps.

I changed the topic quickly. "So, your mom. How old were you when they divorced?"

"Ten, almost eleven. Mom took it pretty hard. He gave her money, but I think…" He shook his head. "She was always sad."

"Right." The conversation was taking a depressing turn, and hearing about their divorce probably wouldn't help me. So I said, "Your place looks neat, how long have you been staying here?"

"Last two years. It's the dumps, you mean."

I laughed. "I was a messy kid myself. But I thought…"

"That I'd have fancy digs?" Leo smiled and shook his head. "This is fine."

"Most kids don't know who your dad is, do they?"

"No. I like being in college, doing my own thing. I know I'll have to go work at the casino at some point, but till then…"

There was a brief silence again. I said, "If Sophia didn't do it, who do you think might…"I let my words trail off. I was asking a kid who he thought might have killed his dad, and he looked so young and vulnerable. I wanted to act like a professional PI, but instead, I found myself worrying about how Leo was coping.

He got up, went to the kitchenette and poured himself some cereal. "Uncle Neil and Dad used to argue sometimes. I didn't think it was serious, but you must've read in the papers how he drove home from the same party but didn't see the car or anything."

"Right. Anyone else? Maybe at work?"

There was a long pause as Leo added some milk and dug into the cereal. "Max," he said. "Max something. He used to be Manager at the Riverbelle, but Dad fired him. One time I was having dinner with Dad and he rocked up unannounced and started yelling stuff."

"What kind of stuff?"

"Don't remember. Dad dragged him off to a different room and they talked some, and then he left."

I nodded, making a mental note.

Leo chomped down some more cereal. "Do you need to know anything else?"

I shook my head, and pulled out my wallet. I put my business card on his table and said, "Call me if you think of anything."

He nodded. "Right."

I turned to leave and said, "You were at a party that night, right?"

"Yeah, at my friend Matt's house. There were fifty other people, there's photos up on Facebook."

"When did you leave?"

"Around three. My friend Kevin lives up the street and he gave me a lift home."

I nodded. Leo did have the perfect alibi. Maybe it was too perfect. "Well, thanks for your help."

I let myself out and sat in the car, jotting down notes and wondering why Sophia hadn't mentioned anything about Ethan's infidelities. It bothered me that she'd left out something so important, and I wondered what else she might have left out.

CHAPTER FIVE

I replayed Nanna's message from the previous night. Her voice was low and I could make out the soft music of slot machines and jingling coins in the background: "Tiffany! You must be at work. I'm at work too. Just met the World's Biggest Sucker - but don't tell your mother."

I smiled to myself and then played the message I'd received this morning. "Tiffany, this is your mother. Call me back when you get this. Your grandmother came home after 1 a.m. last night and I know she's up to something. Has she told you anything?"

Just when I was thinking of maybe calling back tomorrow, my phone rang. It was my mother again.

I groaned, but there was no point putting it off. I summoned up my courage and answered the phone. "Hi, Mom."

"Tiffany." I could hear the disapproval in every syllable, and I pictured her standing in the middle of the kitchen, wearing her 'Mom Uniform' of a floral-print shirt and baggy, high-waisted jeans. "Do you have *any* idea what your grandmother's up to?"

"No, Mom."

"Well." There was a slight pause and Mom lowered her voice. "She came home late last night but I couldn't smell any alcohol on her. I'd be happier if she was out drinking. She said she was playing slots with her friends, but I don't believe that."

"I'm sure she can take care of herself."

"Hmm." There was a pause. "How are you doing?"

"I'm ok."

"Have you met anyone nice? You know, I've been telling you I could introduce you to my friend Kirra's son. He's very handsome."

I groaned. "No, Mom, I don't want to meet him. I told you before." She tried to say something but I interrupted quickly, "Is Nanna around? Maybe she'll tell me what she's doing."

My mom was clearly disappointed at not being able to regale me with tales of how wonderful Kirra's son was. But curiosity about what Nanna was up to won out. "Ok," she said, sounding a bit dejected. "Hang on."

I heard her calling out, and then a long pause until Nanna picked up the phone in her room. "Tiffany, dear."

"Hi Nanna, how are you?"

"Tiffany, I know your mother's listening in from the phone downstairs and I told her specifically not to. I may be old, but I need my privacy. How would she like it if I listened in on her call to Marge when she talked about how annoyed she was tha–"

I heard a soft, disgusted grunt, and then a sharp click. I laughed and I could sense Nanna smiling at me with her sharp blue eyes at the other end of the line. She was pretty quick with her opinions and insights, and despite her wrinkles and white hair, she was a snazzier dresser than my mom.

"So," I said, "How's the poker going?"

"Terrific. You know, last night I was at the Mirage and this hick man from Texas showed up. Played all aggressive at first, so I took him for a ride, and then he tightened up and lost on some big hands. And then I lost a hand to him on purpose, bidding up on a pair of fours, and he thought I was a stupid old hag and started playing too aggressively again. And after that," she finished smugly, "I won some of the easiest money ever."

"Well, good for you!"

I was proud of my Nanna. At seventy-four, she's one of the smartest, most ruthless women ever, and it's a terrible idea to cross her. She's not a Vegas local, but when she moved here a few years ago to live with her daughter she quickly infiltrated Vegas' mafia-like retirees' society, learned all the local gossip, and got the hang of Vegas coupons, slots and comps.

A few weeks back, I thought she might be getting a bit bored. One of her closest friends, Madge, had passed away and Nanna started talking about getting too old to do things. So I introduced her to the world of poker. I was sure she'd be a natural, with her innate talent for math, seeing through peoples' lies, and keeping her own thoughts and knowledge under wraps.

I was right. So far, Nanna had been steadily picking up more skills, playing up her Silly Old Codger persona and, thanks to clueless tourists and drunken locals, slowly increasing her bankroll. According to her, poker was fun, exciting, and of course, profitable.

"How's your love life?" Nanna asked. "Have you met anyone exciting?"

"I'm too busy for that, Nanna. I –"

"You know," she said, "You haven't been with a man in ages. In my day, we used to say, 'use it or lose it.'"

I didn't want to know what 'it' was. Nanna has a gift for the inappropriate, and though she's super-smart, sometimes I dread to hear what will come out of her mouth next. So I quickly said, "Actually, I'm too busy because I got my first case as a PI!"

"Well that's exciting!"

"Yeah, but remember, don't tell Mom and Dad about my PI work yet. I want to be able to close my first real case before I tell them what I'm doing."

"Ok. So who's the client?"

"Sophia Becker."

I heard a sharp intake of breath and then Nanna said, "That old Ethan Becker murder? I never believed for a moment that Sophia was the killer!"

"Really? Because they found the gun in her bedroom…"

Nanna made a noise like a cat throwing up. "That's nothing, something else is fishy. You need to focus on the other suspects, wrap things up fast. This case should be a cinch for you, I don't want you wasting too much time – don't you want me to see my great-grandchildren before I die?"

"Sure," I said, slightly disappointed that no matter what, Nanna managed to turn the conversation back to my non-existent love-life and off-spring. "Anyway, I should say goodbye to Mom and get to work."

I heard Nanna holler for my mother, and after a few seconds Mom picked up. "Well? What's going on with your Nanna?"

"Oh, nothing." I tried to keep my tone light. "I think she's just having some fun with those old friends of hers."

My mother made a strange snorting noise. "That's not much better! You know how much trouble those crazy old hoons can get into."

"I think they're just enjoying some late-night comped buffet dinners. You shouldn't worry so much."

"Hmm." My mother sounded doubtful, and I made a move to hang up before she could start badgering me again about my life, my boyfriend and my career – or my lack thereof of all three. Well, maybe the career thing might improve if I could solve this case.

"Give my love to Dad," I said, "And don't feed Sprinkles so often, he's way fatter than any cat should be."

CHAPTER SIX

I stood at an empty blackjack table, cards spread out in a fan before me, waiting for someone to step up. It didn't take long. The weekend rush continues till Monday at the Treasury, and it was still only Sunday.

I dealt the cards, made some small talk, and dealt some more. Midwesterners in colorful clothes, businessmen on the last day of their holiday, and groups of partying kids came and went, won and lost. I laughed at their terrible jokes, told them sincerely that I hoped they won, and accepted their tips.

I moved between tables and there were times when I had to concentrate – when I was calculating the payouts on roulette or blackjack, when I was trying to charm players into giving me more tips, or when I needed to deal with an angry drunk guy and had to marshal up my meager powers of diplomacy.

But every other moment, when I was alone at a table, on a break between shifts, or working in a zombie-like trance, I thought about Leo Becker.

The kid was cute. I understood why Sophia couldn't imagine him being a killer – he seemed so naïve and sweet and easy-going. It might have been one big act, but he'd seemed too hung-over to pretend. The inheritance could've been a motivation for anyone else, but Leo didn't seem to care much about money.

I quickly ruled out Leo as a suspect and began to wonder about Ethan and Sophia's marriage instead. Had Ethan really been having affairs, and if so, had Sophia known about them? In between dealing cards for a game of PaiGow and coquettishly refusing the advances of an inebriated Asian man, I wondered if Sophia had been hiding anything from me.

After my shift finished, I went home. I stayed up for a long time, unable to sleep. It was my first day on my first real case, and I could feel the anxiety building within me – I wouldn't find anything new, Sophia would be convicted, and I would never get another job as a PI. My own client was hiding things from me and I was terrible at interviewing people. I wasn't tough and cynical enough; why would anyone ever hire me again? On top of all that, I would never meet anyone decent in this stupid town, Nanna would never get to see great-grandkids, and I would die alone – unloved, miserable and a failure.

At some point, I curled up into a tiny ball of neuroses and drifted off to sleep.

When I woke up in the late morning, the first thing I did was to call Sophia and tell her that I needed to see her, would she be home half an hour from now?

"Of course," she said, laughing bitterly, "Where else could I go? I was always the scandalous stripper and now I'm the outcast."

I hung up and raced through my apartment, pulling on jeans, running a comb through my hair and tumbling over myself in the rush to get to my car. In my haste to meet Sophia, I contributed to the speeding problem on the expressway and, like everyone else who was driving above the speed limit, I felt perfectly justified in doing so.

After the previous night's near panic-attack, I was determined to crush through my fears and figure out whatever I could to help Sophia be acquitted. I told myself I could do it, I would focus on one thing at a time, and before long all my work would be finished – and then I would let myself stress over everything else that was wrong in my life.

By the time I entered Sophia's pretentious mansion, I was in a slightly bad mood. I was annoyed at all the expressway drivers who'd been in my way, and at Sophia for hiding facts about her marriage from me. Plus, I was caffeine-deprived.

So after Sophia ushered me into her mansion, I skipped the small talk and announced, "I need coffee and some breakfast."

If Sophia was surprised by my bluntness, she didn't show it. She didn't even make a snarky remark about not being a café – she merely turned around and led me to her large, gleaming marble-and-stainless-steel kitchen where she heated up a blueberry Danish and made me a latte.

As soon as I had two bites of Danish and a sip of coffee inside me, I turned to Sophia and said, "Tell me what you know about Ethan's infidelities."

There was something in my tone that told her not to evade the question. Or maybe it was the wild glint in my eyes, my crazy hair, or just the fact that she wanted me out of her house before I guzzled my way through all of her expensive coffee. Either way, Sophia said, "Before or after I married him?"

"Both." I took another sip of the coffee. "But start with after."

Sophia's eyes drifted downwards and she raised her shoulders in a tiny shrug. "I should've seen it coming. He was rich, he could do whatever he wanted. I had a vague hope that he'd be faithful to me but I guess I wasn't enough."

"When did you find out?"

"Three months after our wedding. He was having one-night stands. Six months later, I thought he might be serious about someone else."

"And then?"

"I was bitter about the one-nighters, but I freaked out about the affair. I thought he might leave me, so I raised hell. As far as I know, he ended it. I reminded him that if I had evidence of the affair, a divorce court would null the pre-nup for me. He got more careful after that."

"But?"

Sophia sighed. "It's not like he stopped seeing the women. He just got more careful. Three months before he died, I was pretty sure he was seeing someone again. But Ethan promised me he'd start getting therapy, and we'd work on making the marriage better." She looked at me seriously. "I don't want you to think he was a bad man or we had an unhappy marriage."

Who was I to judge? The closest I came to romance in my own life was when I bought heart-shaped boxes of chocolate for myself. My last serious relationship had been over a year ago, and I'd come to accept that finding and being with a man you loved wasn't as easy as it seemed in those up-beat romantic movies.

I shrugged and finished my Danish. "I don't care about your marriage. But this does give you a motive for murder. Did anyone else know he was unfaithful to you?"

"I'm sure a few people did."

"Did anyone know you were unhappy about his affairs?"

"Probably. I had a fight with him in his office a few weeks before he died. I thought he was seeing someone there. But he kept telling me we'd be fine, we'd work things out and stay together."

I swirled my tepid coffee around in the snazzy glass latte cup. "Who was she?"

"What?"

"Who was the girl?"

Sophia shook her head. "She could be anyone. A stripper, a friend, someone he ran into on the street."

"But you had your suspicions."

"Yes."

"And?"

"I thought it might be Audrey. This girl I was introduced to, once."

"Audrey who?"

"Audrey Waldgraf." She shook her head again. "But I don't want to make false accusations."

"What makes you think it was Audrey? Who is she?"

"Ethan's casino was being audited…"

I almost spit out my coffee. "By the Gaming Commission? This is *huge!*"

"No. This was an internal audit."

I let out a breath. "Oh."

"Yeah, Audrey's firm was looking at the Riverbelle's accounting."

"Nothing to do with the gaming?"

"No, Audrey worked at Spencer, Tyler and Goldberg, the audit firm Ethan had hired."

"And what makes you think she…?"

Sophia frowned. "Like I said, I'm not sure. But one time when I went to the casino to pick up Ethan, she was there, and Steven introduced us. She was cute."

"And?"

Sophia rolled her eyes. "It was a hunch. Ethan started acting weird again, coming home late, going on strange trips. I caught him with a pair of Cartier diamond earrings one time. He claims they were for a high-roller client, but I'm not stupid. I saw Audrey a few days later, wearing a flawless diamond pendant that cost more than her annual salary."

We sat in silence for a few moments and then Sophia said softly, "The thing that got to me was the *effort* he put in. He's always gone for the low-hanging fruit. He's never bothered to chase someone."

"*I'm* pretty convinced from your story that he was seeing Audrey. Did you ever ask Ethan about her?"

She shook her head. "No, it's not like I saw them together or anything. The first time, before he got careful, I caught him in bed with a woman."

Her voice was dry and cynical, and I stared at her like she was nuts. Which she was. If it had been me, I would have shot Ethan that very first time.

I didn't like my thoughts travelling down that route, so I said, "Tell me about before."

"Well," Sophia said, "To hear him tell it, he never found true love. Vanessa was a good wife, but just not…"

"He told you that?"

She shook her head. "Word gets around. He used to visit the club when he was still married to Vanessa, and strippers talk to their clients."

"That was ten years ago. You wouldn't have been working then."

"No. But rumors trickle down."

"So… he told the strippers he wasn't happy with Vanessa, that's why he slept around?"

"Pretty much."

"Anyone else tell you this?"

Sophia smiled. "When you're about to get married to one of the richest men in Vegas, people will tell you things."

"People who?"

"Leo had dinner with us before we got married. He told me I'd be just like his mom, unhappy with a cheating husband."

"How'd Ethan react?"

"He said Leo didn't know what he was talking about."

Once a cheater, always a cheater. But I didn't know how this information helped in the investigation. So I said, "I talked to Leo yesterday."

Sophia nodded. "Cute kid, right?"

"Yeah."

"You're wasting time talking to him. Any jury'll love that guy. You need to speak to Neil, I'm sure he'll let something slip."

I wasn't quite so sure, but it was on my list of things to do and I might as well get it over with. "Where's the best place to find him?"

"Go to the casino, you can pretend you're there for business or something."

I nodded. There didn't seem to be anything else to talk about, so I thanked her for the breakfast and left.

It took me a stressful half hour to get from Sophia's gated mansion to my humble off-Strip condo. Once home, I reflected on the fact that I was feeling slightly better about my work, incredibly disgusted with Sophia's 'marriage,' and a whole lot more caffeinated. I pulled out my laptop and did some research on the Riverbelle Casino and its employees.

After making a few notes, I dialed Neil Durant's cell phone number and held my breath, hoping he would answer and fall for my plan.

CHAPTER SEVEN

He answered after two rings. "Neil Durant."

"Hi, Neil. This is Tiffany Black, I'm a reporter for the Nevada Times and I was wondering if I–"

"You'll have to speak to my PR officer, she deals with press."

"Natasha Williams? Yes, I've already spoken with her. She said it's best, in this case, if I speak with you directly; she gave me your private cell phone number."

There was silence for a few seconds. Neil must've decided my story added up, because his next words were, "What's this about?"

"Mainly some questions about Riverbelle's future direction. I'd like to speak to you in person about the specifics. Are you free anytime today?"

I held my breath, hoping Neil would say yes.

After a brief pause he said, "I've got ten minutes at 3 pm."

Before I could thank him, he hung up with a click, and I smiled to myself, relieved that my plan had worked, and rehearsed what I'd say in my head.

I drove to the Riverbelle with a few minutes to spare. I wore a black pant-suit, my most expensive Manolo Blahnik stilettos, and a chunky cocktail ring on my right hand. I hoped my outfit somehow screamed 'reporter' and that Neil would agree to tell me something interesting.

The Riverbelle Casino was toward the northern end of the strip, and though the exterior wasn't as flashy as the Bellagio or Ceasar's Palace, it had a clean, modern look. Parking was a breeze and I walked over to the lobby. The large gaming pit was visible from where I stood and had a modestly busy look – if I had to guess, I'd say that the Riverbelle was doing decent business. Not great, but not too bad either for these crazy economic times.

"Hi," I said to the serious-looking man in Reception. "I'm here for an appointment with Neil Durant. Tiffany Black."

He glanced at me, checked something on his computer, and then handed me a blank plastic keycard. "Go left and take the elevator," he said, sounding bored. "Swipe the keycard and press 37."

I thanked him and headed off, noting the security cameras everywhere. There were cameras along the lobby, cameras in the hallways and cameras in the elevator.

I got off on what was obviously a corporate floor, accessible only by those with the right keycards. There was a small reception counter, beyond which I could see an open-plan working area with executives typing away at computers. There were large rooms beyond the open-plan area, walled off by translucent frosted glass. I guessed that the largest room was the security team's workspace and the medium-sized rooms were conference areas and executive offices.

I walked up to the cute blonde working at reception and said, "I'm here to see Neil Durant."

She smiled and nodded. "He'll just be a minute."

I waited on the couch nearby and the receptionist was right – a stunningly good-looking man appeared within a few minutes. We introduced ourselves and I followed him back to his office, impressed that he hadn't kept me waiting long, hopeful about the interview.

Neil looked like he was in his late twenties, but I guessed he was actually in his late thirties or early forties and spent a lot of effort maintaining his ex-model good looks. He was tall, muscular and tanned, with a Botox-smoothed forehead. His hair was dark and slightly long. I promised myself I'd do some more research when I got home and look up photos of Neil modeling underwear.

As I settled into the chair opposite his desk, I noticed he was observing me with an intensity that would have seemed creepy from a less good-looking man. I smiled and said, "Why don't we get started with the interview?"

"Of course. What would you like to ask?"

I pulled out an MP3 voice recorder and placed it on the table between us. Immediately, Neil shook his head. "No recordings."

Damn. I put the recorder back in my purse, but left it playing. Without the interviewee's consent, a recording wouldn't be admissible evidence in a court, but it might help me later when I was putting together my notes.

"The first thing I want to ask," I said, "Is what your future plans are for the Riverbelle Casino."

Neil leaned back in his chair and narrowed his eyes. He crossed his hands behind his head in a gesture of mock relaxation, but I could tell that he was still watching me suspiciously, as though I might suddenly do something crazy like pull a gun on him or jump onto his desk and start dancing topless.

"I have big plans," he said, "But they're private. What's the next question?"

"Uh." I stared at him in confusion for a split second. That first question had been a ruse, intended to get him to lower his guard and start spouting corporate bullshit about how wonderful the casino was and how they would be even more profitable soon. His hostile answer threw me off a bit, and was at odds with how eager he seemed to be to do the interview. I decided to push ahead regardless. "How has Ethan Becker's death affected the Riverbelle?"

His eyes brightened and he leaned forward. "It's business as usual. I was the CEO when he was around, and I made most of the decisions. That hasn't changed."

"And how has Mr. Becker's death affected you personally?"

"I miss him, of course. But that hasn't affected my work or the profitability and future growth trends of the Riverbelle."

"I believe you and Mr. Becker had some disagreements when he was alive?"

"Yes, I didn't always agree with his ideas for the Riverbelle."

"And did you have any disagreements on personal issues?"

Neil shook his head. "I don't see how that's relevant."

"Well – I *am* writing an article about the Riverbelle's past and future, so I'd like to g–"

"Really? Because I talked to Natasha, and she said you never talked to her. And then I called the Nevada Times, and they said nobody named Tiffany Black works for them."

My eyes widened and I could feel the blood draining from my face. I was surprised Neil had even talked to me for so long.

He smiled. "Why don't we get this cleared up? Who are you really working for?"

I kept staring at him in shock. My mind had gone blank and I tried desperately to switch it back on. Why hadn't I planned a back-up identity?

"Alpha Investments? The Warkowski brothers?" Neil mistook my shock for stubbornness and said, "I've had a few proposals already, and you won't get any information unless you let me know who the buyer is."

"Buyer?"

"For the Riverbelle."

Of course. Why hadn't I thought of that? That would have been a great cover. I was about to launch into a story about how I worked for a private buyer, but then I stopped. That wouldn't help me at all – Neil would just talk about financials, and how great he was at his job.

"I'm a private investigator," I admitted. "I'm not working for any investors, I'm just looking into Ethan Becker's death."

It was Neil's turn to look at me in shock, and for one split second I was pleased by his reaction. And then I realized he would clam up, so I quickly said, "This isn't about you. I just have a few quick questions about Mr. and Mrs. Becker."

Neil crossed his arms. "Who hired you?"

"Sophia Becker."

He broke out into a short laugh and said, "That woman thinks hiring you will help her? No way. I can't stand that… witch."

"Uh… I just w–"

"Nope. Not answering any questions."

He pushed his chair back and stood up, indicating that our time was over. Regretfully, I stood up too.

"I won't ask about you," I said. "Please, just give me five minutes?"

Neil rolled his eyes and looked at his watch. "You've got sixty seconds."

It was better than nothing, and before he could change his mind I said, "Can you tell me about Steven Macarthur?"

"Ethan adored him."

"How long has he worked here?"

"Forever. Ambitious guy, rose up through the ranks."

"What about Max – the manager before him?"

Neil frowned. "Max Desilva. Yeah, he was here a long time too, but he left – not on the best of terms with Ethan."

"Do you know why?"

He shrugged. "The usual. Thought he had been wrongfully fired, knew he wouldn't get a job anywhere else. Caused a fuss a few times, but we haven't heard from him in a while."

"Right. What do you know about Mr. and Mrs. Becker's marriage?"

Neil looked away and his gaze grew shifty.

"I know he was always unfaithful," I said. "Was he having an affair with Audrey Waldgraf?"

Neil shrugged. "I wouldn't know."

"Why w–"

He cut me off brusquely. "That's enough. We're done here."

I extended my hand and he grasped it and held on for a second. "I do miss Ethan," he said. "He was a good man and I'd like to help bring whoever killed him to justice. But you're wasting your time working for Sophia. Everyone knows she's a gold-digging stripper. It's quite likely for someone to snap after being miserable for too long, just as it's likely for someone to take the winding way home after he's had a few too many drinks at a party."

He looked and sounded sincere and he let go of my hand, nodding towards the door.

"Good luck," he said and I let myself out.

I handed the keycard back to the disinterested man at reception and felt a pang of hunger. It must've been hours since I had that Danish and coffee at Sophia's house.

"Where's a good place to eat?" I asked the man.

He glanced at his watch. "Now? I'd say the Café de la Rue would be a good bet, if you're looking for somewhere quiet." He pointed down the hall. "That way, first right, can't miss it."

"Thanks," I said, and headed off in search of… maybe some afternoon pancakes, I decided, or a nice chocolate muffin, or maybe a slice of tiramisu, or maybe even –

I was so intent on drooling over imaginary food that I bumped straight into someone.

"Whoops!" I said, "Sorry." And then when I noticed who it was I smiled. "Leo! What're *you* doing here?"

Leo smiled back. "Just visiting the place with my aunt."

That's when I noticed the woman standing beside him. She was a slender, beautiful brunette wearing a leopard-print Diane von Furstenberg wrap dress and red stilettos.

"Oh, hi," I said, extending my hand, "I'm Tiffany Black."

"Thelma Durant. Are you a friend of Leo's?"

"Kinda." I glanced at Leo. "What're you two up to?"

"I'm showing him around the place," Thelma said with a sad smile. "I thought he should know more about it, since he owns half the place now."

I wanted to correct her, that he owned one-third of the place, and Sophia owned the other third. But my recent chat with Neil had made me realize how painfully unpopular Sophia was with her in-laws, so instead, I said,

44

"I was so sorry to hear about your brother. I hope you're doing ok?"

"Yes. We're ok."

"You were home when it happened, right?"

"Yes."

"That's so sad." I was finding it hard to ask her anything else about the murder and still act normal, and I couldn't even think of what to ask her. I glanced at Leo, but his face was blank.

"I guess I should let you two get back to the tour," I said, "It was nice meeting you, Thelma. And good to see you again, Leo." I dropped him a wink, and hoped he understood not to tell Thelma who I was.

I watched the two of them walk away, and moved slowly in the other direction. I passed the Café de la Rue, but didn't go in. I kept walking, thinking about Thelma, wondering why the cops hadn't bothered to investigate her. She had no alibi; but then again, she had no real motive, either. Maybe Sophia was right – once the cops found the gun, they were afflicted with tunnel vision and couldn't see that someone else might have been involved. Or maybe they *had* investigated Thelma and hadn't found anything.

I got to the end of the hallway: there were frosted sliding glass doors, and a sign above that said *Riverbelle Spa*. I retraced my steps, and found myself at Reception again. There was no sign of Thelma and Leo.

"You again," the man at Reception said, mock-sighing. "Can't get rid of you, can I?"

I laughed in what I hoped was a flirtatious manner and tried to bat my eyelashes. "Actually, I was wondering if you'd be able to get hold of Steven Macarthur? The manager?"

The receptionist looked wary. "I know who he is."

"Tell him it's Tiffany from Alpha Investments. I wonder if he could spare a moment? I can wait."

He looked at me suspiciously, then went over to a phone in the corner. I couldn't hear what he said, but I saw him glance back at me occasionally. His entire conversation must've taken five minutes, but to me, it felt like hours and hours. The seconds ticked away slowly and I felt like I'd just made a fool of myself. Finally, when my legs were starting to develop pins and needles, the receptionist hung up and came back to me.

"He's busy," he said.

I wasn't surprised, but I was still a bit disappointed. So far today had been going well – Sophia had talked to me about Ethan's 'lifestyle,' Neil had talked to me despite what Sophia had said about him, and I'd run into Thelma… I'd been hoping my luck would continue, but apparently not.

Oh well, it had been worth trying. I shrugged and headed down to the Café de la Rue. Time to put my original plan into action – what had I finally decided on, pancakes or tiramisu?

Café de la Rue was dark with soft jazz music piping through. The tables were private and secluded and the staff was discreet. It was the kind of place you went to break up with your melodramatic girlfriend.

I ordered a cappuccino and a triple-chocolate cupcake, and settled at a table at the back. When my order arrived, I munched happily, immersing myself in the joys of caffeine and chocolaty moistness. I was mid-bite and drowning in the pleasure that only a triple-chocolate cupcake can bring, when the chair opposite mine was pulled out and a short, stout man sat down.

I swallowed rapidly and stared in surprise. The man had salt-and-pepper hair, a squarish face and puffy jowls. He looked like a bull-dog and was craning his neck forward like one.

"Tiffany from Alpha Investments?"

His voice was dry and I nodded quickly.

"I'm Steven Macarthur. You have two minutes, before I ask you to leave."

Stay calm, I told myself. "I'm here to ask a few questions about your financials," I said rapidly, "Sales, growth projections, that kind of thing."

"No you're not. Ninety seconds."

I stared at him and he stared back. I wondered how he knew – had Neil told him?

"I'm a private investigator. I just wanted to ask a few questions about Ethan Becker and his family. I'm sure you knew him very well."

Steven stood up and pushed his chair back in. "I've got nothing to say to you. The police have done their work and I don't think you should make Ethan's family relive their trauma. I recommend you leave immediately. I've settled your bill."

I watched as the man turned around and walked away rapidly.

What had just happened? Neil had been perfectly friendly to me and there was no reason I couldn't sit and have some food in his café. If Steven didn't want to talk to me, he didn't have to. There was no reason to order me to leave. I appreciated the man's loyalty to Ethan's family, but I had been looking forward to my snack and the cupcake was delicious.

On the other hand, my throat had gone completely dry and I didn't know if I could even swallow any more food. The man wanted me out of here badly enough to settle my bill before coming and intimidating me, and chocolaty goodness or not, my heart was pounding and I needed to get back to the safety of my tiny condo.

I stood up and grabbed my purse, not bothering to look at my half-eaten cupcake. Nobody else had heard our exchange, but I felt the cafe's dark walls pressing in on me, and I walked out, trying to look unconcerned.

The hallway outside was brightly lit and I took a few slow steps forward. I noticed as though for the first time the way the place smelled like lavender and the soft chamber music being played.

There were two men standing in the hallway, looking at each other. They were barrel-chested and muscular, dressed in matching black suits and white shirts. I had seen enough men like them to know they worked in security. I wondered why they were just standing around in the hallway instead of being in the gaming pit, but they stood silent and alert, as though they were waiting for something.

The men didn't bother to glance at me as I walked down the hall, but as soon as I stepped between them, one of them moved forward and wrapped a hand around my forearm. I jerked back instinctively, but his grip tightened and I looked into his eyes. They were small and beady and glittered like tiny dark marbles. He smiled thinly.

I narrowed my eyes and kept my voice steady as I said, "Let me go. I was leaving anyway."

"You're not leaving," he said, in a deep, gravelly voice. "You're coming with us."

CHAPTER EIGHT

Beady Eyes kept his grip on my arm as we headed down the hallway and the other suited man followed right behind. There was no way I could wrench my arm out of Beady Eyes' vise-like grip, so I allowed myself to be pulled behind him.

I wondered if I should scream for help. But the thought must have occurred to Beady Eyes at the same time and he pulled me around in front of him and clapped his other hand over my mouth.

The other man stepped to our left and I slid my eyes to look at him. He had a French-cut beard, a shaved head, and a vacant expression; he was opening a heavy door labeled 'Authorized Personnel Only.' Through the open door I saw a flight of stairs and Beady Eyes shoved me towards it. I walked down the steps, pushed along by Beady Eyes, with Mr. Beard following close on our heels.

The stairs were gray cement and the walls were a dirty white. I heard the door close behind us with a dull thud and a heavy silence descended. Everything down here seemed sparse and from a different, older era. Even the air was thinner, and my throat caught as I tried not to hyperventilate.

Beady Eyes kept his grip on my arm as we descended, but he removed his other hand from my mouth and said, "No-one can hear you down here."

I could feel my heart thumping in my chest, my pulse throbbing between my ears and I gulped, glad the men couldn't see my face. There were no cameras down there and I wondered if anyone knew where I was. But there had been cameras along the hallway. Surely someone on the 37th floor had seen what was going on. But maybe they had seen and hadn't cared. Or worse, they had seen and they approved.

We reached the bottom of the stairs and Beady Eyes pushed me to the right. I walked down the narrow passageway in front of him and Mr. Beard opened a door to our left. Beady Eyes pushed me into the room and let go of my arm.

The two men stood blocking the doorway and I stared at them. Both of their faces were impassive and I thought I caught a hint of uncertainty. They stepped out and closed the door, locking it from the outside with an audible click.

"Wait here," Beady Eyes called through the closed door, as though I might decide to wander off.

I heard their footsteps grow fainter and fainter, until I couldn't hear them anymore.

Once Beady Eyes and Mr. Beard were gone, I breathed deeply and felt my heart slow a little. I wasn't going to die. Not yet.

I looked around the room. It was about the size of Neil's office upstairs. Which is to say, it could fit a dining table that seated twelve people. Not that twelve people would ever want to have dinner in this dingy place.

The walls were a grayish white and I could tell they hadn't seen a coat of paint in the last twenty years. There was a massive rectangular mirror on wall, a small table in the middle of the room, and two uncomfortable-looking chairs. I couldn't see any security cameras anywhere.

I drank it all in and felt a sudden rush of relief: I knew what this place was. It wasn't a place where you took people to brutally murder them. It was a place people could leave with their heart still beating properly and all their organs intact.

This was the holding room. There was one in every casino, from the place where I worked to the grandest of them all. It was customary for a casino to use these rooms as waiting areas for cheats or petty criminals, before handing them over to the police.

Although I'd never seen a holding room without cameras before.

The realization made my heart squeeze tightly and I looked around once more, trying to detect something I'd missed. Nope. No cameras anywhere.

Who was I waiting for? Mr. Beard and Beady Eyes were obviously unsure as to what to do once they'd gotten me down here. They didn't seem like the smartest cookies around and I remembered the look of mild confusion on their faces. Someone else was telling them what to do and they'd probably left me alone to seek further instructions.

I took a deep breath. I was completely out of my depth and didn't know what was going on, but I could handle it. I perched on the edge of the tiny table and rehearsed a speech in my head: "I came here to meet Neil Durant and I would like to leave now." Surely the two buffoons wouldn't dare displease their boss.

But then I remembered how they'd brought me down here despite all the cameras in the hallway. My heart sank. Nobody cared what happened to me.

I waited quietly in the room, my mood oscillating between hopefulness, despair, and terror as I glanced at my watch every couple of seconds.

Almost thirty minutes later, I heard footsteps, and then I heard the door being unlocked. It was opened, and I saw my two old buddies, Mr. Beard and Beady Eyes.

They were both smiling and this time they stepped into the room and shut the door behind themselves. Mr. Beard positioned himself near the door and Beady Eyes walked toward me.

I stood up and promptly forgot my rehearsed speech. "I'd like to go," I stammered. "Neil Durant – I met him, I need to talk to him again." I had a sudden flash of insight. "I'll have to tell him how you two are treating me."

The two men exchanged a look, and I took a step towards the door.

Beady Eyes grabbed my arm immediately. "You're not going anywhere," he said, his voice low and menacing, his fingers digging into my skin. "Tell anyone about this meeting, and we'll deny it, and so will our boss. *Everyone* will deny it."

"Who's your boss?"

"That doesn't matter. All that matters is your co-operation. And we're here to make sure we get it."

I stared at him and my hands went cold. I wanted to ask what was going on but I couldn't speak. I knew that if I opened my mouth, no sound would come out. So I left it shut.

Beady Eyes took another step forward. "So," he said, "Here's what's going to happen. You're not going to come in here, ever again. You're not going to talk to anyone who works here, ever again. And you're not going to investigate this Mr. Becker's death anymore." He bent down so his eyes were level with mine. "Do you understand?"

I nodded rapidly.

"And you agree to all those things?"

Once again, I nodded hastily like one of those bobbing dolls you see on car dashboards, my head moving up and down quickly like it was being pulled by a tight, invisible wire.

Beady Eyes smiled, pleased with my reaction. "Do you know what happens if we find out you're talking to anyone about the casino or Mr. Becker?"

I stared at him and tried to shake my head.

He moved his face closer to mine. I could smell his bad breath and the lingering scent of a cigarette. "We'll make sure you end up like Mr. Becker," he said. "Dead on the side of the road. Or maybe we'll take you out to the desert;

54

more convenient that way. We'll make sure no-one can recognize you. Though it would be a shame to cut up someone as pretty as you."

He moved his face away and let go of my arm before he turned to Mr. Beard and said, "What do you think? Think she'll remember?"

Mr. Beard's face broke into a wide smile. "Nah. But we can make her remember."

Beady Eyes slipped his arm around my waist and smiled down at me. I felt as if I were being choked by my fear.

And then suddenly my brain-fog cleared. I knew what I was going to do. I smiled and tilted my head, lowering my eyelids flirtatiously. I wrapped my arms around his neck and stepped closer.

I watched as the confusion spread over his face, and was instantly replaced with hope and curiosity.

I slid my right leg in between his legs and lifted my knee sharply. It was a high cheerleading kick, except it made contact with his scrotum. Beady Eyes' face went white and his eyes almost popped out of their sockets. His mouth opened in a silent 'o,' and I moved back and let go.

Mr. Beard was still standing near the door, looking puzzled. Out of the corner of my eye I saw Beady Eyes double over in pain, and the other man took a few worried steps towards me. My fingers balled into a fist and my arm swung out. My heavy cocktail ring caught Mr. Beard sharply on his jaw and he let out a muffled groan as he reeled sideways.

Just to be on the safe side, I quickly pulled off one stiletto and rammed the sharp, pointy heel through Mr. Beard's neck. It went straight through his flesh, and the man let out an agonized scream. Blood gushed out in dark, red spurts.

I pulled off my other shoe, grabbed my purse, and ran out of the room. I ran all the way down the corridor and up the stairs, and Mr. Beard's screams continued to echo through the air like the bad soundtrack of a carnival funhouse.

When I got to the top of the stairs, I wrenched the heavy door open and found myself back in the hallway.

I felt like Alice coming back from the rabbit hole. Everything on this floor was unchanged: the place was well lit, the comforting scent of lavender wafted through the air and the chamber music was a soothing contrast to Mr. Beard's funhouse screams. I glanced up at the cameras on the ceiling. There were so many of them, blinking away silently, capturing my every move. I stared up at one in particular, sure that someone on the 37th floor was watching me. I didn't know who it was, but I raised my arm up towards the camera, made a fist and stuck out my middle finger.

I stood like that for a second. Having made my point, I ran down the hallway, past the lobby and out the door. I didn't stop running until I reached my car, jumping straight behind the wheel and tearing out of the lot like a mad woman.

I drove without thinking, taking turns and ramps by instinct, checking my rearview mirror occasionally. My spidey sense was on alert. I couldn't see anyone tailing me, but I couldn't shake the feeling that I was being followed. I swerved and made sudden turns and lane changes, but my tactics didn't seem to do anything but make other drivers honk loudly and yell at me. That feeling of being watched never went away and I wondered if this was what a descent into madness felt like.

CHAPTER NINE

I found myself heading towards Lake Las Vegas and keyed my way into Sophia's gated community. As the automatic gates shut behind me I hoped that whoever was following me, if there was anyone following, wouldn't be able to get in. But I supposed they didn't need to get in to know that I was going to go talk with Sophia.

I called her from my car and she picked up after one ring.

"I'm outside," I said, "Are you home?"

"Yes. I'll get the door."

I sat in the car for a moment and realized that my heartbeat had finally returned to normal. I took a look around. I was safe, alive, and the only casualty had been my poor stiletto.

As I stepped out, I wondered who Mr. Beard and Beady Eyes were working for. It could be anyone – Steven,

58

Thelma, Neil, Leo or even the bored-looking man in reception.

Sophia stared at me from the door as I crossed the driveway barefoot.

"What happened to you?" she asked, barely able to keep the look of disgust off her face.

I pushed past her and headed into the nearest room, the formal living area with its antiques and Persian rugs. "What's your shoe size?" I asked.

I could see in Sophia's eyes that she thought I was on some kind of medication. "Si-ix," she said slowly.

I frowned and shook my head. "Won't work. I'm a seven. I'll buy a new pair of friggin' Manolo Blahniks and bill them to you. Or maybe Jimmy Choos this time."

"Right." Sophia looked at me like I had horns spouting from my head. "Did you come here just here to talk about shoes?"

"No. I'm off this case. That's it. I'll send you my final bill and we're done."

She went pale and bit her lip. "You can't do that. We have a contract."

"I'm terminating it."

"Look." She came and sat near me. "I don't know what's gotten into you but I can't let you quit. You know I'm depending on you."

"Go depend on someone else." My heart was beating wildly again. I knew I was being a coward, but I'd just gotten out of one sticky situation and I didn't know if I'd be so fortunate next time. I didn't like Sophia enough to risk my life for her.

"No-one else will take the case and you know it. What's wrong? Please tell me you smoked something or had a bunch of drinks before you came here."

My voice rose an octave. "Do I look like I smoked something?" Come to think of it, I probably did. I took a deep breath and forced myself to calm down. "No, I'm fine. I quit. I don't need death threats and creepy guys trying to hurt me."

We stared at each other for a few seconds and then Sophia said, "What're you talking about? Who threatened you? Are you hurt?"

"I'm fine." I lowered my voice. "It was Beady Eyes and Mr. Beard."

Sophia looked like she'd choked back a laugh. She smiled and nodded indulgently. "Yes. Of course. Beady Eyes and Mr. Beard."

"Don't smile at me like that! I'm not an imbecile."

"No, of course not." She was using what I supposed was her 'soothing voice.' "Why don't you wait here and I'll get you – what would you like? Black coffee? Fries?"

I stood up, scowling. "I'm outta here. For all I know, you hired them yourself." That option was starting to make a lot of sense. I nodded. "Yes. You hired me just so you could say that to the jury, and then you hired Mr. Beard and Beady Eyes to scare me off so I don't find anything else."

Sophia looked worried and stood up. "I guess if you're on some kind of drugs, there's no point hiring you. But nobody else will work for me. So it's a tough choice."

"For the last time," I said, gritting my teeth, "I'm not high. I drove straight here from the Riverbelle, where I went to talk with Neil and Steven, and two freaky security guys dragged me into the holding room and threatened me. I've been told very specifically to stay off this case unless I want to wind up dead in the middle of the desert and I'd rather stay alive, thank you very much. Sorry about the case…" I trailed off lamely. "I hope you find someone else."

Sophia looked at me seriously. "So you're not high."

I grabbed my head and half-screamed, half-groaned. "Argh!" I felt like shaking her. "Is that all you got from my speech?" It was amazing how I refrained from calling her names.

Sophia shook her head. "You can't quit, I won't find anyone else."

"Well I can't just get killed either, so between the two, it's a rather easy choice for me."

"No, you don't have to…" I could see the wheels spinning in her pretty little head. "You said they tried to hurt you," she said, "How did you get away?"

"Kicked one in the balls and stabbed the other with my stiletto. Which I've lost, by the way. Forever." Sophia burst out laughing and I glared at her. "It's not funny. Those were my favorite pair of Manolos."

She shook with laughter for a long time and then finally managed to get herself under control. "But don't you know any kung-fu or something? I thought all private detectives knew cool fighting moves. You could have just done some karate chopping and saved your shoes."

I took a deep breath. "No. I don't know that stuff."

"Well you're working around bad guys, wouldn't it make sense to know some self-defense moves?"

"Yes, it would." Obviously I needed someone like Sophia to point out how big a loser I was. "But it's a bit too late now. I quit."

"Wait, we can figure this out."

"Nothing to figure out," I said, "I'd like to be able to keep my organs, my life and my new stilettos."

"No." Sophia frowned and sat down again. "You're not just quitting."

I looked at her uncertainly. It seemed kind of rude to leave right now.

Sophia jumped up, as though she'd just had a brilliant idea. I expected her to say something insightful about how I might avoid Mr. Beard and Beady Eyes but instead, she said, "You must be exhausted after what happened. How would you like some hot chocolate?"

I looked at her curiously. Hot chocolate did sound good. Come to think, that was a pretty insightful comment. "With marshmallows?"

"Absolutely."

I brightened up. "Ok."

Sophia led me to the kitchen and as we walked, she pulled out her cell phone and dialed a number. "Stone," I heard her say, "This is Sophia Becker. I have some work for you, it's rather urgent. Please call me back when you get this."

I wanted to ask who that was, but before I could, Sophia said, "Do you want a light hot chocolate or a creamy one?"

It wasn't even a choice. "Creamy."

She nodded and I sat down on a barstool at the counter and watched as she pulled out a milk carton, a jar of heavy cream and a block of dark chocolate. She placed the dark chocolate on a chopping board and pulled out a knife, when her phone rang.

"This is Sophia... Oh, hi, Stone... It's a protection job... No, please don't send Zac, I'd rather talk to you... Sure, I'll see you in ten minutes."

I watched as she put down the phone and began chopping up the dark chocolate block into tiny bits. "Who was that?"

"That was Stone," she said, as though that answered everything.

I wanted to ask who he was, but a part of me didn't really care. I was here for the hot chocolate and when that was finished, I'd leave. I watched Sophia heat up the heavy cream and milk, and add the chocolate and sugar.

"How come you have all this stuff?" I asked. "It doesn't look like you ever eat anything."

She smiled. "I eat. I have a personal trainer and work out two hours a day."

"Right. But you don't eat hot chocolate or Danishes or cupcakes."

"Those are for my friends. Sometimes the girls from the club come and visit me. They're basically the only people who still hang out with me."

My eyes widened. "You're still in touch with them?"

"What? Just because they're strippers we can't be friends?"

Point. "So why'd you become a stripper?"

"Same reason as everyone else. I needed the cash. I figured I'd dance for a few years, save a bit of dough and get a degree. Maybe start a small business."

"But you met Ethan instead."

Sophia smiled. "Yes. I fell for that man like a ton of bricks."

And then found out he was some kind of sex addict. I tried to come up with something nice to say, but I didn't know the man and what I'd found out didn't seem particularly nice. So I said, "You know, the investigation really doesn't seem to be going anywhere. Nobody has anything to say a–"

Sophia cut me off. "Keep trying. Something's gotta come out."

"No, it doesn't really. You know, even the police have unsolved cases sometimes."

Sophia poured out the drink and reached into a cabinet for the packet of marshmallows. She popped two into the mug of hot chocolate and said, "I don't care. Keep looking. Find something."

She placed the mug in front of me and I wrapped my hands around it. Sophia's eyes looked glassed over and her smile seemed to be pasted on from years of practice. She was selling herself a dream in order to stay calm and I wondered what would happen if I couldn't deliver on that dream.

There was a knock on the door and Sophia sashayed over to answer it. I heard muted voices and sipped on my hot chocolate. It was good, just what I needed to make up for losing that triple-chocolate cupcake.

The voices grew louder and Sophia walked back into the kitchen with a man at her side. He was tall and wore jeans and a white shirt. He was muscular in an understated way, more athletic footballer than beefy security guy. His face was serious and angular, and his dark hair fell slightly over his forehead. His eyes were piercing black and I could tell they missed nothing, and when his gaze met mine I felt a sudden rush of electricity.

Sophia said, "This is the friend I wanted you to meet."

He held out a hand and said, "Jonathan Stone."

"Tiffany Black."

We shook hands and he sat down on the barstool next to me. I wondered how he and Sophia knew each other. Had she been his stripper? Had she slept with him? Not that I cared.

As though reading my mind, Sophia said, "Stone did some work for my husband."

Well. That probably meant she hadn't slept with him. I don't know why that made me feel better, but it did.

I turned to him. "What kind of work was that, Jonathan?"

"Call me Stone."

"Stone." The correction made me feel naïve and I frowned.

"I did some executive protection work."

"Oh." That was a euphemism for bodyguard duty.

Sophia prompted me, like she was urging a toddler to recite a nursery rhyme, "Tell him what happened with Beardy and Pointy Eyes."

"Beady Eyes," I said, sounding cross, and took a sip of my hot chocolate to remind myself why I was here.

Stone crossed his arms on the counter and leaned forward, looking at me carefully.

I glanced at him, half-expecting him to smile encouragingly, but his face was impassive.

"I don't know who you are," I said to him, "I'd feel silly telling you the story of my life."

His expression didn't change. But he did say, "What do you want to know?"

"Well, for starters, who you are, what you do, and what your background is."

"Jonathan Stone." There was a long pause. "I'm a guy. I own Stonehedge Security. I was in Special Forces. I'm retired from that now."

"Stonehedge Security. What do you?"

"Security services."

The guy was attractive, but I wondered if he was daft, or just being obtuse. I didn't need an idiot protecting me, but on the other hand, he *had* been in Special Forces. He must've had some experience with men like Beady Eyes and Mr. Beard, and probably with men a lot worse.

I shook my head. "I'm fine. I don't need protection." I picked up a teaspoon, fished out one half-melted marshmallow and chewed it happily.

Sophia was watching us carefully and said, "So you'll keep working on the case?"

I swallowed the marshmallow, fished out the other one, and ate it thoughtfully. Now that I had some warm, chocolate liquid inside me, I was feeling a lot better. Come to think of it, Mr. Beard and Beady Eyes were clearly imbeciles, the way they had let me run off like that. I probably didn't have anything to fear from them, really, and I doubted they'd want to tango with me again. Mr. Beard would most likely spend the rest of his life in mortal fear of stilettos, and Beady Eyes would probably spend a week at home with an icepack pressed against his junk. Besides, I'd never go back to the Riverbelle, so I'd never see those two again.

It would be a shame to let Sophia down and give up on my first case. This nice, hot-chocolate-creating woman would be convicted of a murder she didn't commit and I would be branded a failure. I'd always remember that I'd let down someone who needed my help and I'd probably never get a PI job again.

So I nodded and said, "I'll keep working."

"Great!" Sophia smiled. "I knew it was nothing to worry about."

"Tell me what happened." Stone's voice was deep and serious and he swiveled around to face me, his dark eyes boring into mine.

I was about to beg off, but there was something in his eyes that demanded an answer. He was looking at me as though his whole life depended on hearing my story, so I quickly recounted what had happened, finishing off with kicking Beady Eyes, punching and stabbing Mr. Beard, and running out of the casino.

Stone looked at me the whole time, his attention never wavering. When I finished the story, I thought I saw the hint of a smile on his face. "So. You managed to hurt them pretty bad."

"Well," I said, reflecting, "I could hear Mr. Beard's screams all the way up the stairs and I didn't look back at Beady Eyes, but he didn't seem to be too happy."

Stone nodded. "And then you drove straight here?"

"Yes." I remembered the fear I'd felt and how I'd driven like a maniac. "It felt like someone was following me. But that might've just been my adrenaline rush."

Stone looked at me thoughtfully and then he pulled out his wallet; he took out a business card, flipped it over, and wrote something. He passed the card over to me and I read: *Carla Dubois, KravMaga, 586-3325. Stone: 548-2525*

I flipped the card over. The other side was Stone's business card, with his business name and office phone number.

"Call me if you're in trouble," he said, "And call Carla to schedule a lesson."

I tucked the card into my purse and said, "I'm fine, but thanks."

"I see you're not wearing stilettos right now."

Touché. The man might look like he was made of wax and sounded almost like that too, but he wasn't stupid. I nodded and said, "I'll call her."

"Right. The next thing you'll need is a weapons permit."

"I'm not carrying a gun."

Stone looked at me like I'd lost my mind, but all he said was, "Suit yourself."

"I will." I didn't believe in gun violence and I wasn't about to contribute to it.

Stone stood up and looked at Sophia. "Good seeing you again."

Then he turned and left.

I heard the door shut behind him and said, "He doesn't talk much, does he?"

Sophia shook her head. "He does have a soothing presence, though. I'm glad you're staying on the case."

I wanted to tell her that I'd been calmed down by the hot chocolate's presence, not Stone's, but a few minutes after he left us, I was no longer so sure. I finished my hot chocolate and said goodbye to Sophia. As I drove away, I felt my uneasiness creeping back and wondered how long Beady Eyes' and Mr. Beard's injuries would keep them out of commission. For all I knew, they might be quick healers who would be feeling fine by the following day. And whoever they were working for probably had more beefy men at his disposal.

I made a quick U-turn, drove into a side street and made a full circle around the block before heading back onto the expressway. Despite my fancy driving and the twists and turns I made, I couldn't shake the feeling that I was being followed.

CHAPTER TEN

After all the troubles of the day, my night-shift at the casino went surprisingly well. It was just the kind of pleasantness I needed – by some miracle the tables I dealt at didn't have any drunks, super-grouches or uber-unpleasant people.

I went to bed feeling hopeful and woke up the next morning feeling just as optimistic. I called Vanessa Conigliani straight away and when she answered, I introduced myself as a detective investigating the Ethan Becker murder.

"Would it be possible to meet up some time today to discuss the case?" I asked, and there was a slight pause.

"Around what time?"

"Whenever's convenient for you, Mrs. Conigliani."

She sighed. "Oh, what the hell. Can you come over in two hours?"

Two hours would be a bit of a rush. I hadn't had breakfast yet and I'd been looking forward to a relaxing morning. But this woman was the last person on the list Sophia had given me and I really needed to talk to her. "Of course." I said. "Will you be at the Summerlin house?"

"Yes," she said. I repeated the address Sophia had given me, just to verify that it was right.

We hung up and I rushed to make my morning coffee and get dressed. I was sure Vanessa Conigliani would be a sweet woman, but just in case, I wore my heavy cocktail ring again and my second-favorite pair of stilettos.

Mrs Conigliani's house was a modest Californian bungalow on the other side of Vegas. It seemed warm and inviting on the outside, with a cute, desert-scaped garden; when I rang the bell, Vanessa answered within a few seconds.

She was a slim, petite woman in her late fifties and I hoped I would look so fabulous when I reached her age. Her hair was blonde with a few subtle highlights, cut to just below chin-length, and she wore black capri pants and a white silk top.

"This is a gorgeous place," I said, looking around. The living area was open-space, done in sleek modern tones of white and silver, with low-lying cream leather couches and fancy abstract artwork on the walls.

"Thanks," she said, "I redid it recently. It used to be done up more retro."

I nodded. "Retro is in these days, but I love this airy feel." The wide windows opened to the street and it was obvious she had magnificent taste. Unlike Sophia's mansion, this place didn't have that gaudy, opulent vibe, but it was clear that Vanessa had sourced the best things she could find.

"You should do interior design for a living," I said, and she laughed modestly.

"Maybe someday," she said, "If I keep feeling this bored."

I looked at her curiously. Sophia hadn't told me much about the woman and internet searches hadn't turned up anything either. "What do you do with your time?" I asked.

Vanessa smiled and sat down, indicating that I should do the same. "I used to own a hairdressing salon. But I sold that two years ago and I've been trying to find something else to keep myself busy. Dealing with hairdressing clients got frustrating. I can't imagine doing the same thing with interior design clients."

"Yes," I mused, "I imagine they'd be picky."

She shook her head. "You have no idea. The women who hire designers are just so… I don't know. Something. Demanding, unrefined, spoiled."

We smiled at each other with perfect understanding. I liked this woman.

"So, Mrs. Conigliani–"

"Please, call me Vee, everyone does."

"Of course. Well, as I said, I'm here about Ethan Becker's death. I think it would be easiest if we started with what you said to the police when they talked to you."

Her eyebrows went up a fraction of an inch. "I thought you were working for the police."

Right. I'd told her I was a detective, without mentioning that I was a *private* detective. Impersonating an officer was a federal offense, so I quickly said, "No, I'm a private investigator, looking into it."

"Who hired you?"

"Sophia Becker."

"Oh. Well. I'll try to help you, but to be honest, I think she did it. I've never really liked her and I think she must've gone nuts living with him."

"I understand he was quite the philanderer."

Vanessa smiled wryly. "Oh, that's an understatement. I was such a fool to marry him. I got pregnant with Leo before I could do anything, and then I stuck it out for another ten years. I still can't believe I stayed for so long."

"Was the divorce tough?"

She shrugged. "All divorces are tough."

We sat silently for a while. "It must have been difficult, raising Leo by yourself."

"It wasn't easy. I was lucky Ethan didn't try to swindle me out of money. He paid my fair share in the settlement, and he paid alimony. He was a decent dad, I'll admit. He didn't try to worm out of responsibilities, so I think Leo dealt with it ok."

"I've met Leo. He seems like a nice kid, you must be very proud."

Vanessa smiled. "Yes, he's sweet."

"I'm sorry to keep coming back to this, but Mr. Becker's behavior? How long were you married before you discovered he was being unfaithful?"

Her gaze drifted into the distance. "That was almost fifteen years ago… I really was in love with him, I didn't care about his money or the casino or anything. Maybe that's why it was so hard for me to believe he was cheating on me. But now I know he was probably only faithful for a few months. Just the first few months, until he got bored."

"Who would he… who do you think he was seeing?"

She laughed drily. "Anyone who would sleep with him. He was the easiest man to seduce, he loved the low-hanging fruit and the women who wanted to please him. Didn't care if it was a stripper or an attorney."

"Must've been tough."

Her eyes locked on mine. "It was."

A chill went down my spine. Despite Vanessa's restraint, I knew she was unburdening her soul to me in her own understated way. I could imagine all the heartbreak she'd been through, and in the fickle crowd she mingled with, she'd obviously had no-one to share her woes with.

I changed the topic quickly. Ethan Becker was dead but I couldn't help dislike the man intensely.

I said, "When was the last time you saw him?"

"I'll tell you what I told the police. I saw him a fortnight before his death; we were having a family dinner with Leo. We do that once in a while, maybe once a month, once every two months. I don't know how his marriage was with Sophia. I didn't ask him those things. We stuck to neutral topics, the weather, sports, and how Leo was doing." She paused and thought back to what she'd told the police. "You'll want to know where I was that night - I was home. I'd gone out for dinner at La Mamba and I left around eleven. I was home the rest of the time. Ethan and I were on relatively good terms, as good terms as you can be ten years after a divorce."

I nodded. "Do you have any idea who he might be seeing now?"

She looked at me with an expression of mild surprise. "What do you mean?"

"Sophia thinks he was seeing someone and it might have been serious."

"Did she have any particular suspicions?"

I shrugged. I didn't want to lead her on. "Not really. Do you have any idea?"

A moment passed as Vanessa tried to think. Finally, she said, "When we were married he used to visit the Peacock Bar. It's the strip club where he met Sophia. I'm sure he kept going – maybe a girl there?"

I nodded. That made sense, but I was more inclined to think that he would sleep with a young auditor who he saw at his office every day. So I said, "How about anyone at his work?"

Vanessa frowned. "I know Ethan liked his women, but I'd like to think he kept some things off limits."

"What makes you think that?"

She shrugged. "I don't know. I don't know anything about him, really, come to think of it. Even our marriage was a lie."

She sounded bitter and I hated to bring up the past. But I needed to get information and she obviously needed to get things off her chest. I might as well take advantage of that. "You mean the philandering."

"Yes, that. Even after all this time…" She bit her lip and then went on. "The man was an enigma to the public, but I thought he love me. He shared things with me. We really connected on so many levels, but then he…"Her voice trailed off.

"Did you try counseling?"

She shook her head. "He didn't believe in those things. These days you would call him a sex addict, but I think it was more than that. He needed adoration as much as he wanted sex."

"It must have been a tough choice to leave him."

She nodded. "I can imagine why Sophia would kill him. You can't stay because he drives you nuts, and you can't leave, because you're giving up that whole lifestyle."

"But you left."

"It was a tough choice. All his friends shunned me and his family stopped talking to me. I had to start from scratch. There were times when I was bitter, but I moved to Summerlin, made new friends. I guess it all worked out in the end. And I have Leo, too. I guess I should be thankful."

I understood the loneliness emanating from the woman. Giving up your whole social circle must be tough. But that was good for me because she was the first person, other than Leo, who was actually telling me things I needed to know.

"So you think Sophia did it?" It was more of a statement than a question.

"I guess. She gets his money *and* she doesn't have to live with him? Sounds like a win-win to me."

"Except she didn't win."

She nodded. "Yeah. The gun. But that was a fluke. I think without that she might've gotten away with it."

I bit my lip thoughtfully. "You don't think she'd be sad to see him dead?"

Vanessa laughed drily. "Does she look sad to you? I know, she hired you and all that, but the woman…" She shook her head. "I don't want to bad-mouth your client, but you gotta admit she's a stripper who married a rich man for his money. I don't think for a minute that she loved him, or that she cares about his death. She's probably happier now."

I frowned. I liked the fact that she was talking to me, but I couldn't bring myself to agree with her. Something about Sophia made me think she was innocent. Or perhaps it was just my naïve hopefulness.

"What about Thelma Durant?"

Vanessa twisted her lips. "She was reasonably friendly when I was married to Ethan, but after the divorce either Ethan poisoned her against me, or she never really liked me to begin with." Her voice trailed off, slightly sad. "Anyway, she seems nice enough. But who knows."

I nodded and stood up. I couldn't think of anything else to ask her, so I handed her my card. "Please call me if you think of anything else."

"Of course."

She walked me to the door and I noticed her watching me curiously as I got into my car. I waved and drove away.

Despite her willingness to talk, I hadn't learned much from Vanessa, but at least she had given me the idea to go check out the Peacock Bar.

Nothing had turned up so far, and maybe the strip club was worth a shot.

CHAPTER ELEVEN

I parked near the club and called Sophia. "I'm about to enter the Peacock Bar," I said, "Do you know anyone I can talk to?"

"I'll call Dan and tell him to help you. He's the DJ."

We hung up, and I walked slowly to the entrance. I hoped Dan would know something, because if he didn't, I was at a dead end.

The Peacock Bar was a little west of the Strip and had a large, street-facing façade, But the main entrance was in a side-alley: all the better for the patrons' privacy. The darkness took a few seconds to get used to when I stepped inside, but the pulsing music and laid-back vibe made me feel welcome. There were a few lingerie-clad girls on stage, moving their bodies lazily and a few others were wandering around the men sitting alone at tables. This was a slow time for the club, but even at its busiest, it would never get as crazy as some of the really big Vegas clubs. The Peacock

Bar prided itself on being more 'classy,' but that was really just a euphemism to say that they were more expensive and wanted richer patrons.

I got a few curious glances from some of the girls as I headed over to the DJ booth. As I neared, the DJ looked up with a friendly smile. Dan was a big-boned guy with a crew-cut and he looked like a suburban dad who'd cheer for his kids at their soccer game.

He took off his headphones and pressed a button to make the music keep going. "You must be Tiffany," he said and I smiled.

We made introductions and small talk, and then I got down to brass tacks. "I heard Ethan Becker used to come here quite frequently."

Dan nodded. "The man would bring clients, business associates, investors – he thought the club brought him good luck."

"Any particular girl he liked to see?"

Dan thought for a while and shook his head. "Hard for me to tell, I'm usually concentrating on the music."

I wondered how he could ever do that with all the eye candy wandering around half-naked.

He caught the eye of a nearby girl and she wandered over with the grace of a dancer. I wouldn't have been surprised if she really was a dancer – a lot of the Los Angeles starlets and dream-chasers became Vegas strippers when they needed extra cash.

"Tiffany, this is Milli," Dan said. I smiled at her.

Milli was tall - even without her six-inch heels - with long, wavy brown hair and big doe eyes. She was curvaceous and poised, with a magnetic aura that made me think she'd do well on stage. I introduced myself and told her I was a private investigator looking into Ethan Becker's death.

"Do you think he might've been having an affair with anyone here?" I asked.

Milli shook her head. "If he'd been seeing someone, he wouldn't have come in so often. They'd just hang out somewhere else."

I nodded. "Did you know him?"

"Yeah, I gave him a few private dances. The guy didn't talk much, but he told me was married and had a special mistress."

"What does that mean, special mistress?"

She shrugged. "He seemed to think she was a big deal. But it wasn't anyone here."

"Did he talk about anything else? Work, any hobbies?"

"He didn't seem to have any hobbies apart from women. And he brought in people he worked with, but they never talked business."

"Right." I tried not to look disappointed. "Well, thanks. You guys've been a big help."

We said our goodbyes and I left, my heart sinking with each step. Nothing was going how I'd expected – but what had I really expected? That Neil Durant or someone else would just confess to killing Ethan and then I'd be done with my work?

I headed over to a nearby café and sat in a quiet corner with my notebook. I replayed my conversations with everyone and began making notes, hoping that things would come together at some point. I jotted down who said what and made a few notes about Mr. Beard and Beady Eyes.

When I'd finished, I knew no more than I had when I'd first started the investigation. It was late afternoon when I put my things away with a sigh and drove back home.

I stepped out the elevator and walked right up to my door before I noticed that something was wrong. The door was open just a crack. I'd definitely locked up before I left this morning.

My heart began thudding loudly and I pushed the door open. Standing out in the corridor, I called out. "Hellooo? Anyone there?"

There was no response.

A chill ran down my spine and I tried to take deep breaths and calm down. I needed to think logically, I needed to figure out what to do. Maybe I'd just left the door open by mistake. Or maybe there was someone inside, waiting for me to step in. My hands felt like ice and I could feel the blood freeze in my veins.

I took one cautious step inside. Things seemed to be normal. And then I turned around. The wall above my couch was freshly graffitied with red paint, and it spelled out: *Die, bitch*.

I screamed and ran out of my apartment.

I ran all the way to the elevator, took it down to the lobby, stepped out and just stood there. I was too scared to step outside and I was terrified of going back to my apartment. I was doomed to spend the rest of my life in the lobby.

And then I remembered Stone. I fished his card out of my purse and called him.

He answered after the first ring. "Yo."

"This is Tiffany," I said, "Could you come over to my place please?"

There was a pause. "You ok?"

"Yes, but my apartment isn't."

He didn't say anything to that, so I gave him my address and he hung up.

I stood in the lobby for what seemed like an hour. Just when I thought I'd start introducing myself to the other residents and opening the door for them, Stone walked in. He was wearing a white shirt and jeans again, but when he stepped closer I could tell that his clothes were crisp and nice-smelling and definitely not the same ones he'd worn yesterday. But they looked exactly the same and I wondered if he had a wardrobe stacked with the same shirts and jeans.

It was tempting to throw myself at him and indulge in a soothing hug, but Stone was clearly not the hugging type, so I kept my distance. He nodded at me and as we walked towards the elevator, I glanced down at his feet – black dress shoes and black socks. Wasn't that what he'd worn yesterday? For all I knew, he was probably wearing the same style of underwear, too. Not that I was thinking about his underwear.

"Thanks for getting here so fast," I said, but the sarcasm missed him and he merely nodded.

As we stepped out into the hallway, he noticed my wide-open door, and said, "You left it like that?"

"Yeah. I figured anyone who walks into an apartment with 'Die Bitch' painted on the wall is welcome."

"Know everyone who lives here?"

"Hardly. Tenants keep changing each week. A lot of the condo owners bought right before the crash and then became desperate to relocate."

"Wait here."

Stone left me standing in the hallway and walked into my place. He had his gun drawn and I could see now how it might be useful to have some firearm training. I heard him move about, opening doors and windows, probably checking under my bed. I thought back to whether I had any dirty underwear lying around or not and decided I didn't. It was the usual mess that a single person makes, but I didn't think it was too bad.

"All clear," he called, and I walked in and locked the door behind me.

Stone was standing in the middle of the room, looking around. "They trashed the whole place," he said, "But I've seen worse."

My face turned red and I scowled. "The living room's fine. It's always like this."

He looked at me in surprise. "But you look so neat." His eyes drifted from my head to my toes and then back up again. "Clean clothes and all."

"A few dirty dishes and scattered cushions don't make a mess."

He shrugged. "But they were looking for something. The bedroom's definitely been trashed. All the stuff in your drawers is pushed to one side."

"You looked through my drawers?"

"It's my job."

I stared at him, aghast, and then went into my bedroom and looked around. The laptop was lying on the floor, the screen smashed and wires sticking out from behind the keyboard. Stone had closed my dresser and nightstand drawers, and I opened them. He was right. Everything was pushed to one side. Several things had been tossed on the floor.

My knees suddenly felt like they were made of jelly, and I sat down on the bed. Stone watched me from the bedroom doorway and I said, "You're right. The place *was* trashed. Just not the living room."

"My faith in your sanity has been restored."

His voice was dry and I cracked a smile. "Was that a joke?"

"I don't make jokes."

But the corner of his lip had curled up a little and he came and sat beside me on the bed. I tried very hard not to fall back in exhaustion. All I wanted to do was to huddle into a ball and quit this stupid case, but apparently if I did that, Sophia would be doomed. Just yesterday, I'd made up my mind to be a successful PI who solved her cases, not some loser who gave up when things got tough. More importantly, giving up at this stage wouldn't deter whoever had been painting in my living room.

The thought flashed through my mind that Sophia might be behind all this. Maybe this was all an elaborate ruse to make her look good during her trial. I got off the bed and picked up my laptop. It was a slow old thing and there were times when it frustrated me and made me want to throw it on the floor, but now someone else had taken that fantasy away from me.

I sighed. "How well do you know Sophia?"

A few long seconds passed and I thought maybe Stone hadn't heard me. But then he answered. "I worked for Ethan when he got a few death threats. He seemed to think Sophia was beautiful and smart. That's all I know of her."

"Who sent him the death threats?"

"Some crazy dude who thought Ethan was causing his bad luck in Vegas. Few months later, he was arrested for stalking a movie star. He's in an LA prison now."

I found an empty shoebox and stashed the laptop in it as best as I could. I'd drop it off tomorrow at Electronics Zone and they could send it to their battery recycling program.

Stone stood up. "Did you go to the Krav Maga class?"

"I didn't have time."

"What're your plans for tomorrow?"

"Uh…"

"I know Carla's free in the morning. I'll make an appointment for you at eight."

"Eight?! That's not when people should be up i–"

"And then we'll go get your gun license."

I shook my head. "I'm not doing any of that."

"Sophia's paying me to keep you alive and I intend to make my life easier. What are you doing for the rest of the night?"

I frowned and then remembered. "I'm having dinner at my parents'."

"Great. I'm coming with."

I took a step back in horror. "No way! If you want to help, you can stay here and put things back in the drawers."

"I don't know where they go." He looked at me disapprovingly, as though if only he knew, he could help me stop being such a slob.

I sighed. "Do you have to stick with me?"

"Don't you want me around in case they pull your car over and shoot you? Or make you drive to the desert?"

The prospect of either of those two things was almost better than the prospect of having to introduce Stone to my parents and Nanna. Almost.

"Fine." I rolled my eyes and let out an exaggerated sigh. "But you're not going to say anything."

"I don't intend to."

"Good." I glared at him ineffectually. "Now, if you'll excuse me, I have to take a bath and clean up after my slobbish ways."

Stone moved into the living room and looked at the writing on the wall. "Don't open the door. Keep your windows locked. Call me when you want to leave."

He walked out and I rushed to lock the door behind him.

CHAPTER TWELVE

Now that Stone was gone, I actually missed his presence. Maybe the man did have a point – maybe I did want him around. For my safety, of course.

I made sure all my windows were locked and even opened my closet and checked under the bed. I tried to tell myself to calm down but it didn't work.

I started to draw a bath, but strange noises kept making me jump up. First, it was the upstairs neighbor hammering something. Then, it was a car backfiring. I'm sure a lot of the noises were also in my head but, either way, I couldn't imagine getting naked and having a bath. I removed the plug after a few minutes and the water chortled away. When I thought about having a shower, scenes from *Psycho* began to play through my mind and I cursed myself for being a Hitchcock fan.

Finally, I contented myself with tidying up. I put things back in my drawers, and arranged them the way they used to be - neatly. Ok, maybe a bit more neatly than they used to be. I even fluffed up the cushions on the sofa and collected all the garbage, empty Chinese containers and packets of cookies that were lying around. Damn Stone and his impossibly high standards of tidiness. I didn't even know the man and he was already getting on my nerves.

I packed a bag and called Stone.

He answered before the first ring finished. "Yo."

"I'm heading downstairs. Will you meet me in the lobby?"

"Yep."

He hung up abruptly. The man wasn't a talker, but that would probably be a good thing when he met my parents.

Stone was standing in the lobby, watching an elderly couple as they headed towards the elevator. I smiled at them and they nodded back.

Stone gave me a quizzical look. "Know them?"

I shook my head. "No, but they seemed nice. People come and go in this building. Mostly old people though. There's something about this building that attracts the old-fashioned."

Stone grabbed my arm and frog-marched me out of the building and across the street. "Ow!" I said, "That hurts! You don't have to drag me."

He didn't say anything, but he pulled out a remote key and unlocked a nearby silver BMW convertible.

My eyes widened. Stone opened the door, and folded me inside.

When he slid into the driver's seat I asked, "This is your car?"

The answer was obvious to anyone but an idiot and Stone just looked at me. "Where to?"

I gave him the North Las Vegas address and he programmed it into his GPS. The car slid out of its parking spot and Stone took the ramp onto the I-15, heading north. After a few minutes on the freeway, he suddenly took an exit and merged onto the expressway, heading west toward Summerlin. I was still thinking about how I'd introduce Stone to my parents and by the time I realized we were heading west instead of north, Stone was already merging onto Summerlin Parkway.

I frowned. "Where are we going?"

Stone kept looking straight ahead and abruptly took the Ansari Drive exit. If it hadn't been for his GPS, I wouldn't have known where we were and it struck me that I didn't know who Stone was or where we were heading.

Just when I was about to panic, Stone took a sharp right onto Trailwood Drive, drove to the roundabout, and got onto the Parkway again.

"You're being followed," he said, as though he was complimenting me on my hair. "This is how you throw them off."

I frowned and looked back, as though I could see anything now. "How do you know?"

"I know."

"Hmm." I chewed my lip a bit. "How do you throw them off? I tried to swerve and change lanes."

Stone remained silent. "No, really. How do you throw them off? I guess I should learn this stuff."

Stone glanced at me and I thought his face looked a bit pinched, as though the thought of having to say more than three words hurt. He sensed my persistence and shook his head.

"Pros use two or three cars to do mobile surveillance," he said, "So you gotta throw them all off. If you speed up, usually there's a surveillance car up ahead that'll tag you, and if you just take a sudden turn, the one or two cars behind you will follow. So take a turn to throw off the car ahead, then lose the cars behind you in local streets, then get back on the expressway. By the time you do this, you'll only have one car on your tail, so you just speed up a bit, change lanes, and lose it."

I nodded as though that made a lot of sense. Which it did. But I worried that when it would be my turn to use all those tricks, I wouldn't be able to pull it off. I sighed and tried to give myself a mental pep talk: I could do it, I could do anything.

But I felt my spirit sinking as we pulled up in front of my parents' house. Stone got out and waited for me on the pavement. My legs felt like lead but I managed to join him and I trudged up the short driveway and rang the bell.

Nanna opened the door instantly. She must've been hovering nearby, taking advantage of the fact that my dad was probably glued to the game and Mom was stuck in the kitchen. Sprinkles, our ginger cat, was also watching the door, and she stared at Stone and me for a few seconds before padding away disdainfully.

"Tiffany, sweetie," Nanna cooed softly as she gave me a hug. "And who is this young man? You didn't tell me you've got a new boyfriend. What wonderful news!"

"He's just a friend, Nan. How are you?"

She frowned. "Good. But your mother's getting suspicious so…"

"We'll have to tell her at some point."

"Hmm." Nanna peered carefully at Stone, taking in his clean, well-pressed clothes and angular face. "He's taller than the other ones," she whispered loudly to me and I groaned silently, hoping Stone hadn't heard.

"Tiffany's here," Nanna announced loudly, as though we'd just walked in. "And she's brought a *boy* with her."

I rolled my eyes, feeling like I was back in junior high school. My parents had moved into this house a few years ago, when Nanna had moved to Vegas, and they'd decided they wanted a larger, more modern house. They bought it during the time of massive foreclosures and their new suburb in North Las Vegas was large and safe and new. Not having to go back to the house I grew up in was both a relief and a regret.

My dad left his game and my mom left the kitchen to come and stare at us.

"Hi," I said weakly, and my mom came forward to give me a quick hug and peck on the cheek.

"Hey sweetie," my dad said, "Who's this?"

"I'm Jonathan Stone," Stone said. He leaned forward to shake hands with my parents and gave Nanna a kiss on the cheek.

My parents exchanged a glance and Dad turned to Stone and said, "I was watching the game. Why don't you join me?"

Stone looked at me and then glanced at my mom. "Are you sure you don't need any help in the kitchen?"

My mom was obviously trying not to burst into tears of joy. "Oh no, we're fine," she said. And then she added as an afterthought, "Why don't you ask Tiffany to give you a tour of the house."

Right. That reminded me. "Mom," I said, holding up my bag, "Can I go take a shower before dinner? I didn't have time before coming here."

Mom frowned and looked confused, but she said, "Sure. You can use the guest bath upstairs."

Stone seemed unfazed by my parents' curiosity and he grabbed a seat to watch the game. Nanna and Mom headed into the kitchen to add finishing touches to the salad, and I trailed after them.

"He seems nice," Mom said, her eyes almost wild with hopefulness. "We thought you'd never find a nice guy."

I half-snorted. "You haven't even talked to him."

"Yes. But he offered to help in the kitchen. And he came with you. And he *exists.*"

She had a point. But I smiled, shook my head and said, "He's just a friend."

Mom and Nanna looked at me with frozen expressions of half-hopefulness, half-disbelief. I glanced from one to another and said, "I'm sorry. We're not dating. He's just a friend who, uh, I thought I'd bring along."

"Really." Mom crossed her arms, ready to start the interrogation, and Nanna tilted her head.

"Well," I said quickly, before they could start, "I gotta go take that shower."

I just about raced up the stairs and out of earshot and I said a silent prayer that Stone and I would make it through the night ok.

I emerged from the bathroom about twenty minutes later. I'd taken my time, hoping I would be too late for the interrogation and that food would be on the table when I got back downstairs. I went straight to the den, expecting to see my dad and Stone sitting in silence and watching the game, performing that unique man-ritual I didn't understand.

But instead, ESPN was on mute and they seemed to be having a fascinating conversation. I could hear Stone's voice and see his lips moving, which was surprising in itself. Dad was nodding and as I got closer, I heard him ask, "So, just any kind of regular battery?"

Stone nodded. "The electromagnetic waves look like a brilliant white light and if you put it in on your head and cover up with a hat, no-one can tell who you are."

"That's brilliant!" Dad turned to me and said happily, "Stone's been telling me about surveillance cameras and how to spot them. Now I can get past one without having them recognize me."

"Uh-huh." I wasn't quite sure why he needed to do that, unless he was preparing a grand art theft or bank heist. But I didn't want to put a damper on his spirits, so I said, "That sounds lovely."

I sat down next to Dad and he put an arm around my shoulders and peered at me carefully. "Are you ok, sweetie? You look a little... worried? Tense? Is everything ok at work?"

"Everything's fine, Daddy. Mom says you've been busy."

"Yeah." He sighed. "Just a few clients. And I've been trying to get someone to set me up a website. They say that's the wave of the future."

I didn't think anyone would Google 'plumber, Las Vegas,' when their pipes burst, but you never knew. I thought of the geeky young kids who were turning up to the Treasury these days and all the people glued to their tablets and smart phones.

"And your mom and I are thinking of taking a holiday," he went on, "Maybe a cruise for a month or so. Get away from all this heat."

I smiled and nodded enthusiastically. "Sure. Nanna can come and stay with me!"

Dad narrowed his eyes and peered at me suspiciously. "You two are a bad influence on each other."

I laughed. "Oh come *on*, Daddy! It's not like I'm helping her skip school or something."

"Hmm."

Dad wasn't too unhappy when Nanna moved in. She was always nice to him, she grew fresh herbs on the kitchen windowsill despite the Nevada heat, and her cooking was better than Mom's. However, tales of her exploits with the Old People's Gang got back to him, and I got the impression he was going to say something about Nanna's recent nocturnal adventures when Mom appeared in the doorway.

"Dinner's ready," she announced and we all trooped into the dining room.

Mom said a quick Grace and we began helping ourselves to the roast chicken, grilled veggies, salad and mash. Stone was silent as he dug in, as was my dad. I think they'd exhausted themselves with their five minutes of conversation and it was my mom's turn to try to extract information out of Stone.

"So, Jonathan," she began, but my dad interrupted.

"He prefers Stone."

Mom looked at him in surprise and Stone swallowed the mouthful he was chewing. "It's kind of a nickname," he explained.

"Oh." She looked at him and took a moment to understand. "What do you do?"

"He works in security," I said quickly, "He has his own security company."

Nanna and Mom shared a glance. They weren't sure whether they should be impressed because he worked for himself, or whether they should be worried because he might be bankrupt.

I could see my mom trying to figure out a way to politely ask how his business was doing, but Nanna beat her to it.

"Are you broke?" she said.

Stone said, "No."

"Oh. I thought maybe you were eating here because you have no money," Nanna said.

Stone shook his head. "I have money."

"Stone drove me here in his BMW," I said quickly, and then immediately regretted my words.

My Mom and Nanna looked far too impressed for their own good. So I added, "It's a rental."

"No, it's not," Stone said, and I glared at him.

"Well," Nanna said. "Tiffany drives a car that's older than me."

Stone nodded politely and Mom and Dad laughed at her joke.

"So, Stone," my mom started again. "How long have you had your own company?"

"Seven years."

She nodded. "And what did you do before that?"

"I was in Special Forces."

Mom and Nanna exchanged another smug look.

I put down my fork in exasperation. "Will you guys stop? He's not my boyfriend, he's just a friend."

"Well." My mom looked at me sharply. "Excuse me for being friendly."

If that was friendly, I wanted to know what a KGB interview looked like.

Nanna turned to Stone. "Why aren't you her boyfriend? You're not gay, are you?"

Stone shook his head and Nanna continued. "Not that I'd mind if you were gay, every girl needs a gay boyfriend. You could give Tiffany a makeover. She needs one."

I groaned. Stone looked at me and then back at Nanna. "I'm not gay," he said. "So I can't give her a makeover."

Nanna looked at him carefully. "But you're a snappy dresser."

"Thank you," Stone said.

"I bet you could pick out better clothes than Tiffany does. She dresses like a nun."

"I do *not* dress like a nun!"

"Did you grow up in Vegas?" Mom interrupted.

Stone nodded. "Yes."

"Well." My mom searched about for something else to ask. "Are your parents still alive?"

Stone shook his head. "No."

"Oh, that's a shame. Do you have any brothers or sisters?"

"*Mom!* Let him eat." I was scared Stone would bolt, leaving me stranded here.

"That's ok," he said, "I've got a brother."

"What does he do?"

"He's in the army."

"Is he married?" Mom asked. "Does he have any kids?"

Stone shook his head. "No."

Nanna said, "Is he a baby daddy? I heard these days young men become baby daddies."

For the first time, I saw Stone smile. "No, he's not a baby daddy."

"Why not?" Nanna said. "Is he also gay?"

"I'm going to watch the game," Dad declared. "You coming, Stone?"

"Yes, sir."

The two heaped some more chicken and mash onto their plates and walked off. I had a vague feeling they wouldn't watch the game and would instead talk about evading cameras and blind spots in surveillance systems.

As soon as they left, Nanna and Mom focused on me with laser-like precision. I raised an eyebrow at Nanna, trying to convey psychically that if she bugged me, I would spill the beans on her poker-playing. But clearly, my wordless communication failed. Either that or she knew I was bluffing.

"Why aren't you dating him?" Nanna said. "What's wrong with him?"

"Yes," Mom said, "You should be dating him."

I shook my head. "It's not like that. We're just good friends."

Nanna snorted. "We used to be good friends in my time. But things are more modern now, and you can be 'friends with benefits.'" She peered at me hopefully. "You're not 'friends with benefits' are you? Because if you are, then I understand."

I shook my head. "He's not my type."

"He's your type," Mom said, "You're twenty-eight, every man who's single is your type. You should've gotten married three years ago. Do you know, my friend's daughter Christine has a nine-year old son now? Imagine that! I could have had three grandkids."

She sat there glumly, imagining her three grandkids running around, and I tried to think of something to say that would make her feel better.

Nanna beat me to it. "Cheer up," she told my mother. "Sometimes having grandkids is a disappointment."

"Nanna!" My eyes rounded with surprise and disappointment. "Is this because I didn't get you that iPad last Christmas? You know it's only because Mom told me not to. She thought you would use it to go to adult websites or buy crap online or try to hack into the FBI."

Nanna glared at Mom. "I saw what you bought off eBay last week. And you're lucky I don't tell Peter."

Mom's jaw dropped. I thought for a few blissful seconds that I was off the hook, but then she turned to me and said, "Is it because you're scared of getting hurt? Because you know dear, you have to take a risk sometimes."

I groaned. "No, Mom, it's not that."

"Well. Does he have a girlfriend?"

I didn't know if he did, but I nodded my head vigorously. "Yes, he does."

"Hmm." Mom frowned, possibly regretting all that effort she'd put into dessert. "Well, you're too old to wait for him to leave her." And then she brightened visibly. "You know, my friend Rebecca has a son who's a bit older than you. You remember Sam?"

"The kid who told everyone his parents were aliens from outer space?"

Mom frowned. "No, this is another Sam."

"I'm pretty sure Sam the Alien Kid had a mom named Rebecca."

Mom glared at me silently and then she cheered up. "Well. Nina's nephew will be in town for a visit and I know he's a lovely boy."

She got up and began clearing up plates without asking me if I wanted another serving.

When she was out of sight I narrowed my eyes at Nanna. "You're meant to be on my side," I hissed.

"I am on your side," she said. "He's a lovely young man. All handsome and such. I think you two could have beautiful children someday."

"We're not having beautiful children," I said, "I don't even want children. They're snotty and they scream and they break all your nice things."

Nanna looked at me carefully and then said, "You know, I found a great website online. It teaches you how to seduce a man and steal him away from his girlfriend. I figured I might need those tips someday, but I can pass you the link, if you'd like."

"No, I'm fine."

"Well, then." She leaned closer and lowered her voice an octave. "My friend Dave gave me this program. You install it on Stone's computer and it'll monitor everything he does and you can enter his email and such. Maybe send his girlfriend a mean email or something."

I looked at Nanna in shock. "You haven't used it yet, have you?"

She shook her head. "I'm tempted to see what stuff your mom says about me in her emails, but so far I've resisted."

"Good," I said, "Stay strong. I don't want you arrested for hacking."

Nanna looked offended but just then Mom called out to the guys that dessert was being served. They reappeared at the table and Mom brought out a chocolate lava cake. My favorite. There was vanilla ice-cream to go with it, and I dug in.

I vaguely heard my mom quizzing Stone about something or other – How old was his brother? How had his parents died? What did they used to do for a living when they were alive? Where abouts in Vegas had he grown up? Did he know Tony Kozlowski?

Stone's answers seemed to make Mom happy, but I could tell that my dad wanted to ask him more about evading security. Sometimes I worry that Dad doesn't have enough hobbies.

At some point, I couldn't possibly stuff any more cake into my stomach. I helped Mom and Nanna clear the table, before we all said goodbye. My parents and Nanna seemed sadder to see Stone go than me. I took comfort in the fact that Sprinkles deigned to come downstairs and rub against my legs before we left but she completely ignored Stone, which made up a little for the fuss my family had made over him.

CHAPTER THIRTEEN

When we got onto to the freeway, I said, "Well, that was interesting."

Stone didn't say anything in response, so I assumed he'd temporarily exhausted his conversational skills.

When we neared my place, he said, "Call the Treasury and cancel your shift."

I stared at him. "How do you... Who told you I work there?"

"I looked through your phone when you were in the shower."

"You looked through my *phone*?"

Stone didn't take his eyes off the road.

"Why did you go through my phone?"

"People sometimes hide things. If I'm going to do my job properly, I need to know about you."

"I have private stuff on my phone!"

"Like what? Your texts with Nanna?"

I glowered at him but he continued to look at the road impassively. Although he did have a point. I have no life, so I don't really have private stuff. Still.

"So you looked through my phone while talking to my dad?"

Stone nodded. "He can't seem to tell phones apart."

"No," I agreed sadly, "He can't."

Stone wasn't saying anything and we'd left the freeway. I called my floor manager at the Treasury, Joan, and told her I had stomach flu. She didn't seem to believe me, but she didn't seem to care much, either. Apart from Mondays and Fridays, weekdays were usually slow in the pit. They wouldn't miss me.

Stone took an early exit and then took a roundabout way to my place. He walked me from his car to the building and then came upstairs with me.

"What now?" I said.

Stone looked around. "You've tidied up."

I nodded.

"You need a bolt for the door," he said, "Anyone can work off the security chain."

Well that was heartening to know.

"Would your neighbors mind a bit of noise at this hour?" he asked.

"They'd mind noise at any hour. Probably more now."

"Don't want you staying here till that door's fixed."

I crossed my arms and looked at him, waiting to hear what he'd propose.

"Way I see it," he said, "You can stay here and me or Zac can stand guard outside your door. You can spend the night at my office, or you can check into a casino."

"You mean a hotel."

Stone raised an eyebrow ever so slightly. "You don't think it's the same thing in this town?"

I didn't answer him since he'd already made up his mind about the livability of 'casinos.' Checking into a hotel would cost money, but spending the night in Stone's office would be awkward. And if he or Zac sat outside my door, my neighbors would probably call the cops and have them dragged away.

I sighed. "I don't want you around all the time. I need to interview suspects and such and it's easier if I'm on my own."

He shrugged. "It's ok."

"I guess I should go to a hotel."

"Good choice. Leave me a key to this place and I'll have one of my employees come in and fix it up for you."

I stared at him wide-eyed. It had never even occurred to me that you could fix a problem so easily. I'd envisioned hours of work, a lot of mess with paint, and irate neighbors. Not to mention dangerous goons who'd probably try to interrupt my painting. With my luck, they'd turn out to be artistic goons who didn't like their handiwork tinkered with.

As I packed a tiny suitcase, Stone waited in my living room, flicking between channels on my ancient TV .

"It's just for one night, right?" I called, and Stone grunted in response. I suppose that meant 'yes,' but I packed a few extra clothes just in case.

Stone made no comment when I emerged with my heavy suitcase. We locked the door behind us and got into the elevator.

A woman rode down in the elevator with us. I said hello and managed to identify her correctly as Betty from 516A, one of the tenants who'd been living here for more than a few weeks. She was pleased I'd remembered her and beamed in our general direction.

"It's so lovely to see a young couple going away for a romantic break," she said. "Nowadays everyone gets divorced after a year. That's not what the Lord says is right. How long have you two been married, dear?"

I said, "We're not married."

Her smile disappeared into a thin, straight line and she looked at us sternly. I thought she was going to give us a lecture about living in sin, but before I could explain, the elevator reached the lobby and she strode out, impatient to get away from the reprobates.

Stone and I were on and off the freeway before I could even work out what direction we were going. We did a few circles and then headed back to the Strip. Stone drove up to the Himalaya Resort Casino, and handed his keys over to the valet.

We walked up to Reception and Stone said, "We'd like a suite."

The petite brunette – Vera, if her nametag was to be believed – smiled at us. "Certainly, sir. Would you like a junior, executive, VIP, honeymoon, or Presidential suite?"

Stone turned to me. "What do you want? I'll bill Sophia for you."

I tried not to smile too hard. "I don't want to be too greedy, so not the Presidential. And Honeymoon might be depressing since I'm single. I'll take the VIP suite."

"Great choice," Vera said, and began to reel off a list of amenities that came with the suite. Stone gave her his credit card details and we collected our key and walked up to the room.

It was breathtakingly glamorous inside. I admired the bed, the clever lighting, the massive private hot tub, the fridge full of complimentary drinks, and the view out the window. Stone checked the door and the window, and declared the place to be safe.

"I'm off," he said. "I'll fix up your place tomorrow and I'll pick you up from here at ten. Remember you have Krav Maga at eight. Cab it there and back."

And then he was gone.

I spent a few hours enjoying a leisurely glass of Bollinger while watching a 'reality' TV show about women who had no idea about the real world, then soaked in the hot tub for a bit. I thought about calling Sophia to tell her about the vandalism at my place and that I'd moved in here for the night, but then decided not to update anyone.

I was exhausted by the day's events, and as soon as I snuggled against the soft hotel pillows, I sank into a deep, dreamless slumber. I woke up at dawn. It was a strange sensation, since this was the time of day when I would usually leave work and call it a night.

I had hoped to sleep in a bit longer, but now that I was awake, I decided to make the most of it. I changed into my swimsuit and did a few laps in the pool, and then I headed over to the breakfast buffet where I showed an incredible amount of restraint by only ordering the pancakes and a mushroom omelet.

I went back to my room and busied myself looking over my case notes till half past seven, before hailing a cab outside.

I got to Carla's a few minutes early and was incredibly glad I wasn't late. Carla was a short, slender woman, but she emanated a fierce, intense energy that would make any thug in a back alley flee from her. She could have been anywhere between thirty and sixty and had the agility of a teenager, teamed with a strong French accent.

She introduced me to her plastic dummy, Kevin, and showed me a few basic moves. Kicking the groin, bringing a knee up to the groin, punching the groin. Lots of unpleasant things to do to the groin. It was followed up with unpleasant things to do to the eyes, the little fingers, the neck and the forearms.

Next, Carla introduced me to her assistant, Louis, and showed me how to get out of various holds. Louis was wearing street clothes for this section, and I practiced the moves with him for a few minutes.

After that, Louis changed into a fat suit, and it was time to practice all those dangerous groin-attack moves on him.

I wondered how much Carla was paying him for it, and tried to keep my punches and pokes mild.

"You must be angrier," Carla urged me. "You must remember that this man will rape you, kill you. Think of the ex-boyfriend that said you were ugly. Or the woman who stole the dress in your size from the sample sale. Think of all those things that make you angry. Now focus on Louis, who is weak and terrible and trying to kill you. Also he has just told his girlfriend that she is fat."

I punched Louis in the gut and he fell backwards.

"It is because of the suit," Carla explained, "In real life he will bend forward from the waist, and after that you can kick him in the groin or punch him in the neck and run away. Remember to always run away."

I thought about Mr. Beard and the way he screamed. I felt reasonably confident I could make him scream like that by using my bare hands now. I just had to remember that he told his girlfriend she was fat.

Carla gave me a timetable for her classes and insisted I come again to improve my skills. "Otherwise," she said, "You will be the weakling, the girl who cannot fight."

I nodded and thanked Louis, who smiled at me.

"I felt nothing," he said, "You must punch harder."

Stone picked me up from the hotel at exactly ten. I wasn't surprised that he was so punctual – he seemed to me like one of those obsessive types who plan their travel time down to the last second, using fancy software to calculate drive times compared to current traffic conditions. Or maybe he'd just parked round the corner and camped out in his car for the last five minutes.

"I've upgraded your locks," he said, "So it's safer now."

"So no-one can break in?"

"A skilled guy can pick just about any lock, and you can buy laser cutters that'll cut through any lock."

"Well I feel much better, thanks." Once again, the sarcasm seemed to miss its target.

"When you're inside, you can use the new bolts to be safer. You'll have time to call 911 if someone starts cutting with a laser. Or you can use your new Krav Maga skills to punch them and then run away."

I sighed. It was better than nothing.

Stone looked over at me and said, "From now on, stop wearing fancy purses. Get something you can sling over your shoulder. When you enter your condo, push open the door from the corridor. Look around, then walk in. If the lounge is empty, check the bedroom, then the bathroom. If you're careful, you can spot any intruder. Run for the door, run down the fire escape, and wait on the next floor."

I wished I didn't have to take orders from Stone, but I didn't say anything. His plan sounded good. He parked the car and we went upstairs, and he demonstrated to me how to open the door and look around.

While he was showing me how to peer around the corner to see if there was an intruder in my bedroom, I checked my wall. The red paint was gone, but I knew it was still there, behind all those coats of eggshell white.

Stone showed me the new bolts and told me I shouldn't keep so much junk food in the house.

I was about to make a smart retort when he said, "Now, let's go get your gun permit."

I stood staring at my feet for a few minutes. Stone gave me time to think and after a while I grabbed my purse and followed him out.

I sat silently in his car as we drove towards the police station.

"It'll take a few days to process," Stone said, "But once we get it we'll head to the shop and buy you something."

I didn't say anything. *It's not like I need to actually use the gun*, I told myself. And besides, everyone in Vegas had a gun. Once you headed out towards the desert, you'd be crazy not to have a gun for protection.

CHAPTER FOURTEEN

After I'd completed and submitted the application for a gun permit, Stone and I spent a couple of hours at the gun range, where I shot at targets and learned about grip, stance and aim. It was satisfying to fire at an enemy who was harmless, anonymous, and made of paper. I actually enjoyed myself and I wondered if I'd come back to the range again. If I was to become any good with a gun in real life, I'd need lots more practice, and it was starting to seem worthwhile.

The drive back home was uneventful and we stopped by the electronics store to return my old laptop and buy a new one. Stone walked me up to my condo.

We stopped outside my door as I fiddled about in my bag for the key.

Stone said, "I've shown you how to do the walk-through, so you do it this time."

I nodded, and turned the key in the lock. I stood in the hallway and pushed the door open, like Stone had shown me. I knew that when I did this on my own, I'd be pretty terrified, but it was hard to feel more than a smidgen of fear when Stone was standing right beside me.

I had kept the light on when we'd left, and my condo seemed void of intruders, so I stepped inside carefully. The answering machine was blinking, but I ignored it – it was probably my mom or Nanna, asking about Stone. I couldn't see anyone in the open-space living-dining-kitchen area, but there might just be someone hiding in the bedroom, so I called out, "Helloooo?"

I heard a noise behind me like a puppy sneezing, so I turned to look at Stone. His eyelids were half-closed and his eyebrows were raised a fraction of an inch – he had the look of a tough guy who wanted to puke because he'd just seen someone giving their lover a red rose.

"What's wrong?" I hissed. "You look like you wanna hurl. Too much dinner last night?"

"Why are you saying 'hello' to your intruder?"

I gave him an offended look. "I'm not saying hello. I'm warning them that I'm home. You know, in case they want to run away before I get to them or something."

"They don't want to run away, they're waiting for you. And they already know you're home! They heard you opening the door."

That made sense. "Right." No saying hello, then.

I lifted my left arm to my side like a ballerina and took a careful step towards my bedroom.

"Wait."

The word sounded like a soft bark and I froze in place. "What's wrong?"

"Why're you holding your arm like that?"

"So I can turn quickly. You know, it'll help me keep my balance and stuff."

Stone didn't say anything else, but my arm was starting to ache, so I dropped it and walked over to the bedroom door. I stood with my back against the wall, and peered around. There was no-one in the bedroom.

I let out a sigh of relief and stepped inside. Stone was right on my heels. I was about to head over to the window, which overlooks my tiny balcony, but Stone grabbed my arm.

"Check under the bed first. The order is, bed, closet, window, bathroom."

I nodded, dropped into an inelegant crouch and peered under the bed. "No-one here," I said softly.

"Didn't think so," Stone said. "It's disgusting under there and full of junk."

I frowned at him. "Under-bed storage is efficient."

"It's disgusting, it's dirty and it's bad Feng Shui."

My eyebrows headed up towards my hairline. "Feng Shui?"

Stone looked as impassive as ever. "Chinese decorating method."

"I know what it is." I'd heard about it on feminine interior decorating shows, and once on Oprah, as a method of cleaning your chakra. But those two words were the last thing I'd expected to come out of Stone's mouth. "How do you know about it?"

"Learnt when I was in Beijing on a stealth mission."

Well, that made sense. I opened the closet door and peered inside. Nobody. I just couldn't get over the fact that Stone knew what Feng Shui was. "And now you know all about Feng Shui."

"Of course."

I walked over to the window and pulled the drapes apart. There was nobody on the tiny balcony in front of the window. "And you think my place has bad Feng Shui."

"In pretty much every way. You've got a mess under your bed, so your Feng Shui love area is all messed up. You've been single for a while."

It was my turn to make an angry, wordless noise from deep inside my throat. I started to say something and then stopped. I didn't even know where to begin. I wasn't single because of bad Feng Shui, I was single because I hadn't met anyone. The guys I liked didn't like me enough, and the guys who liked me enough weren't really my type.

But I didn't know how to explain all that to Stone, not that it was any of his business anyway, so I satisfied myself by glaring at him sternly. It didn't seem to make a difference though. My angry stare bounced off his calm, neutral expression, and I headed towards the bathroom. I opened the door and peered inside – no-one in there.

I sighed and looked back at Stone. "I guess you can go. And I can continue with my messy Feng Shui and messy life."

A corner of his mouth twitched slightly. "I didn't say I believed in the Feng Shui effect stuff."

"Oh? So you think my love life might improve?"

"That's up to you. But I still think your place is dirty and messy and you should clean it up."

I narrowed my eyes and wondered if I had anything handy to throw at Stone. Unfortunately, he didn't wait for me to find anything, and before I knew it, he turned around and left, pulling the door closed behind him. I satisfied myself with glaring at the door and imagining the sterile, unfriendly place Stone must call home.

Once Stone was gone, I checked through my place once more, and made sure that all the doors and windows were locked properly. After I'd ensured that my tiny condo was as fortress-like as possible, I played the two messages on my answering machine. They were both from my mom, wanting me to call her, so I sighed and dialed the number.

"Tiffany," Mom said as soon as she realized it was me, "How are you?"

"Good," I said, trying to keep the wariness out of my voice. My mother never called just to ask how I was.

"Have you seen Stone again?"

I knew where this was going, but I didn't want to lie. So I said, "Yes, I have, and he's just a friend, Mom. He's not my type."

"He seems to like you. You know, he came over to meet your parents and have dinner with them. For most men, that's a big deal."

"He doesn't like me, Mom. He's just a friend."

"Then why did you bring him to dinner?"

"I can't bring a friend over to dinner now?"

"I don't remember the last time you brought a date. I guess most men don't take you seriously enough to meet your parents. And we all liked Stone."

I groaned. "Just because you like him doesn't mean I have to."

"Hmmph. Here, your father wants to talk to you."

I heard my dad's voice in the distance. "What? No, I don't want to do this."

My mother must not have learnt the trick of covering the receiver, so I heard her hiss, "Talk to her. It's your duty. Do you want her to end up unmarried and single when she's fifty? Maybe she'll get desperate and marry a no-good deadbeat like Mary's daughter did, and then she'll get divorced and we'll have to sell our house to pay for her divorce settlement and help her raise her kids as a single mother. Do you want that now? Do you?"

I let my head sink into my hand as I waited for my dad to shuffle over to the phone. After a while I heard him say reluctantly, "Hi Sweetie, how are you?"

"I'm ok, Dad."

"Er. Yes. Well." There was an awkward silence and I knew my mom was standing there with her arms crossed, glaring at my dad. "Well," he said again. "You know we all liked Stone. Pleasant young man. Very, um, interesting to talk to."

"He's just a friend, Dad."

"You know, your mother's worried that you're not settling down."

"I kn-"

"I'm worried too."

I imagined my mom must have prodded him into saying that, and I sighed. "I'm ok, Dad. You know lots of girls get married late these days. It's ok. I'll meet someone."

"Er. Ok."

I heard my mom in the background saying, "What's she say?"

"She'll meet someone later," Dad told her. And then he spoke into the receiver again, "I have to go, Sweetie. Your mom wants to talk to you."

The phone was passed back to my mom and she said, "What's all this talk about meeting someone later? You've already met a perfectly nice man. Why can't you just settle down with him? And why can't you dress a little bit nicer when you're around him? Would it hurt you to put on some lipstick sometimes?"

I made my hand into the shape of a gun, and pretended to shoot myself. If I protested, Mom would keep giving me advice. When I was younger, I'd tried to reason with her, but at some point I'd seen the light. Just nod and agree, I'd learnt, and she'll let you go.

So I said, "Sure, Mom, I'll think about it. Hey, I have to go now, Stone's calling my cellphone." A little white lie never hurt anyone.

"Oh." Mom sounded vaguely suspicious and a tiny bit hopeful, and after I quickly asked about Nanna – "She's taking a nap. Out all hours of the night, no wonder she sleeps during the day. Turning into your regular old vampire…" – I hung up and went about getting ready to get to my 'real' job.

I arrived at the Treasury a few minutes early for my shift. I got tired of hearing "Tiffany! I thought you were sick!" and having to explain that it must have been a 24-hour bug. I could tell that nobody believed me, but nobody really seemed to care, either.

The night brought with it the usual parade of partiers and jackpot-seekers. Towards the end of my shift, I wondered if Beady Eyes' boss would try to attack me in the casino, but when I looked up, seeing the glittering domes of the security cameras that littered the ceiling reassured me.

However, I wasn't looking forward to walking back to my condo. I've always had to cut through a few patches of darkness on my way home, and today I regretted not driving in. Thankfully I was able to bum a lift off a gay co-worker and we chatted happily on the short ride back to my place. It was nice to spend some time with a man who didn't answer in monosyllables, and when we got to my building, I invited him up for a drink. He said no, but since he was homosexual I didn't have to feel offended. Maybe he just didn't like my personality.

I tried to keep my spirits high as I headed upstairs, but my heart was thumping loudly and my knees felt wobbly. My door looked untouched and I opened it the way Stone had shown me. I held my breath and walked in slowly, ready to bolt at the slightest hint of an unfriendly presence. Nobody in the living room, nobody in the bedroom, nobody in the closet, nobody in the bathroom. Great. I started to breathe again and went back and locked the door, using the two new deadbolts Stone had installed.

I slept fitfully that night, waking at the slightest sound and then dozing off again. After a few hours, I gave up and decided to get to work.

Over a mug of steaming coffee, I replayed my interviews and made notes. So far, I still had to talk with Audrey and the ex-manager of the Riverbelle. I hadn't interviewed Thelma yet, but that wasn't something I was looking forward to or thought would be particularly fruitful.

Sophia had told me that Audrey's firm was called Spencer, Tyler and Goldberg, so I looked them up online and found their phone number. The office was in downtown Vegas, but there was no list of employees, so for all I knew, Audrey had switched jobs and was somewhere else. Still, it was a start, so I grabbed my phone and dialed the digits.

A woman answered after two rings. "Spencer, Tyler and Goldberg."

"Hi," I said, feeling slightly unsure. "Could I please speak to Audrey Waldgraf?"

There was silence for a moment and then the woman said, "I'm sorry, *who?*"

Maybe the woman was a new employee. Maybe I had mumbled. "Audrey. Waldgraf? I was told she works here?"

There was another long silence. I thought maybe she'd wandered off, but then she said, "Please hold for a minute."

Her tone was serious, and a Mozart concerto began to play. I waited for my call transfer to go through, counting the seconds and wondering if Audrey would agree to talk to me.

Five minutes later, the music stopped and I heard a man's voice. "This is Eli Stark."

I frowned. "Um, hello Mr. Stark. I was hoping to speak to Audrey Waldgraf?" I said her name clearly, hoping I'd be transferred correctly this time.

There was a brief silence and then the man said, "I'm sorry, who are you?"

The interrogation annoyed me. I said, "I'm an old friend of hers."

There was another silence, and then he said, "Really. How old?"

This conversation was getting weird. Did they talk to everyone that way? I wondered how they ever got any business. And didn't they know it was rude to ask a lady her age? "I'm twenty-eight."

"No, I meant, when was the last time you spoke with Audrey?"

"Not for a while," I said, "I was told she worked here so I was just hoping to speak to her for a minute."

"Oh." There was another uncomfortable pause and then the man said, "I don't know who you are but I can't transfer you to Audrey."

"I understand she must be busy at work now. Is there a better time I can call? Does she have a direct number?"

"Audrey Waldgraf hasn't come into work for the past two months. She passed away."

I felt like I'd been hit with a brick.

"Hello?" Eli said. "Are you there? Who is this?"

I came back to Earth. "I'm sorry. My name is Tiffany Black. I wasn't aware…"

"I'm sorry for your loss, Tiffany. We all miss her."

I racked my brain furiously. Audrey had died two months ago, just a month, or maybe even a few weeks, after Ethan had been killed. Surely it couldn't be a coincidence. "How did this happen?"

"Her apartment was broken into and she was just in the wrong place at the wrong time. I've very sorry Ms. Black."

I could see he was trying to wind down the conversation so I said quickly, "No, thank you for telling me. I should've found that out on my own." I remembered reading about a burglary and murder in the paper a while ago, but it was a tiny news item that hadn't gotten much coverage, and it hadn't mentioned any names. "I'm not sure how I missed that, but…"

"Would you like me to give you her parents' phone number? I'm sure I can find it here somewhere."

I took a deep breath. "Actually, I'm sorry to have misled you. I'm a private investigator looking into Ethan Becker's death and I thought Audrey would know something. I didn't realize she'd been killed."

"Oh."

"Mr. Stark, would you mind if I came in later to ask you a few questions?"

"Uh – please, call me Eli. I'm still… surprised by this… I'm not sure I can help you."

"I'm not sure either, but I'd like to talk to you and then maybe get Audrey's parents' number."

I could just about see him shrug. "Alright then. I'm free at ten-thirty, can you drop by then?"

I thanked him and we hung up. I dug out my new laptop and searched for news of Audrey's death. After a few unsuccessful attempts, I finally managed to find her obituary and the news item, and I pieced together the information. Audrey Waldgraf had lived in one of the older apartments east of the UNLV campus and two months ago her apartment had been broken into. The suspect had picked her lock, expecting the place to be empty, and police theorized that when he'd found her home, he'd panicked and shot her. Her place had been vandalized, and it had been unclear what was missing.

The whole thing gave me the creeps. I wasn't sure I believed that it was a burglary or an accidental murder – sure, it could have been a coincidence, but something about the story rubbed me the wrong way.

I sighed. I'd wanted to avoid doing this, but there was no way I could put it off any more. I took a deep breath and called Emily Sinclair.

She picked up after a few rings, sounding relatively cheery despite the stress I knew she was under. "Hey Tiff, what's up?"

"Um, not much. Are you free for drinks this evening?"

I heard the rustling of papers. "Sure. You doing ok?"

"Yeah, I'm great."

I picked a bar near the Tremonte and we decided on the time we'd meet; then she said goodbye and rang off abruptly. I guessed she was busy and didn't take any offence – I was used to her habits by now.

The drive into the downtown business district was a quick one and I managed to find parking only a few blocks from Eli's office. The office itself was in a modern steel-and-glass building, the interior just as shiny and impressive as the outside. I waited for only a few minutes before Eli Stark came out.

He shook my hand firmly and said, "It's nice to meet you, Tiffany."

Eli Stark was a tall, balding man with a mustache, glasses and a perpetually confused expression. He seemed to be constantly thinking of tax deductions and legislations as I followed him into his small office.

He offered me a choice between coffee and water, and when I refused both, he jumped straight into business. "What's this about?"

I took a deep breath. "Audrey Waldgraf was investigating Riverbelle Casinos, right?"

Eli looked puzzled. "Yes."

"There was a rumor she was sleeping with Ethan Becker."

He leaned back in surprise and shook his head. "No, no. That's not allowed, you can't fraternize with the auditee. Sleeping with them is out of the question."

I noticed Eli wasn't wearing a wedding band and said, "But people do have feelings. She might have fallen in love."

Eli frowned and rubbed his chin. "I can't imagine that. I thought she'd be doing great things. She was a hard worker, intelligent, and she was promoted very quickly. I don't think she'd jeopardize her career."

"But people do fall in love."

He stared at me as though he was just starting to recognize that love might be a valid reason. "I suppose so," he said slowly, "But then she'd have to give up the project to someone else."

"Was she working on it alone?"

"Yes, it was a straightforward audit, just checking the books and making sure it was all done according to standards. Audrey said she didn't need any assistance."

"Do you normally have one auditor per project?"

"Yes. Although Audrey could've asked for help if she thought she needed it."

"Not if she was ambitious, I guess."

"Well, the project was cancelled after Ethan's death."

I raised an eyebrow slightly. "What do you mean?"

"Let me check the files." I watched him slide his mouse around and click and scroll, and then he said, "Ah, yes. Here it is. Ethan Becker approached us for the audit. But after he died, the Riverbelle's board voted to put the audit on hold. They thought it was unnecessary at that time, and we refunded them half the money and stopped the process."

"So Audrey was put on a different case?"

"Yes, there was a large project requiring three auditors – a local supermarket with complicated discounts and markups – she was moved to that one."

"Maybe she was going to declare her relationship with Ethan Becker and then the case was closed. So she didn't need to tell anyone."

Eli looked unhappy with my prognosis, but agreed reluctantly. "That could be true."

We sat silently for a few minutes, and then I said, "Did Audrey talk about the Riverbelle Casino's audit with anyone? Was there anything unusual about it?"

Eli shook his head. "She didn't say anything when she was working on it, although those days she spent most of her time in the casino. Auditors tend to work on location and Audrey rarely came into the office. And then afterwards, she was working at the supermarket."

"So she might have discovered something and not had a chance to tell anyone."

Eli shrugged. "It's possible. Anything is possible, I suppose."

"What happened to her files?"

"For the Riverbelle project? There are backups in the office. I'd offer you a peek, but that would break client confidentiality codes and there's nothing to see, really."

I nodded and couldn't think of anything else to ask, so Eli handed me a contact sheet with Audrey's parents' names, phone numbers and address. I thanked him for his time and help, and went back to my car.

CHAPTER FIFTEEN

I sat in my car for a couple of minutes, looking at the numbers Eli Stark had given me. I held my cell phone in one hand, trying to psych myself up to call Audrey's parents. I needed to talk to someone else about her, about what might have gotten her killed. But I just couldn't bring myself to call her parents.

I could imagine all too clearly the heartbreak they must be going through. I couldn't call them up and poke at their wounds; I didn't want to ask them whether their daughter had been having an affair with a married man. I'd been hired to do a job, but I couldn't do that. I put the numbers and cell phone away and stared into space, imagining the person Audrey Waldgraf must have been.

Eli had said she was ambitious and hard-working. It sounded like she could be attracted to Ethan, but only if he'd agree to leave his wife for her. There was no proof she'd been with Ethan, but her death bothered me. I couldn't believe it had been a burglary gone wrong. This seemed more like the kind of thing a jealous wife would do.

I drove home absent-mindedly and glanced at my watch just before I stepped into the elevator. It was almost lunch-time. I could kill some time by making lunch, doing my laundry and taking a shower. Then I'd review my notes and what I'd learned so far, and go to my appointment with Emily.

The fact that it was broad daylight was making me feel bolder than usual, but I still opened my door carefully, the way Stone had shown me. It swung forwards and I took a step in, into my living room.

Immediately, the hairs on the back of my neck stood up. The living room was empty, but I could just feel someone else's presence. They must be in the bedroom. The bedroom door was open, but the bedroom blinds were drawn and the room was in darkness. At this angle, I couldn't see in and someone could be hiding there.

Or maybe it was all just my imagination. "Hel-lo-o," I called out softly.

There was no response. I could hear no movement, no breathing. And yet, I was sure there was someone inside.

I glanced at the wall above my sofa, remembering the red paint that had been there just a day ago. If someone was in my place, they would be either in the bedroom or in the bathroom. They could be in the closet, but that seemed unlikely.

Little things jumped out at me. Had the curtains been rearranged? Maybe the cushions looked a bit off?

I glanced down at my coffee table and saw the ugly vase I had bought at a flea market, years ago. It wasn't much of a weapon, but I picked it up and crept quietly towards the bedroom. I stood flat against the wall and peered around the door. And that's when I saw him.

Standing in the far corner was a man in black, hiding in the shadows. His face was covered with a black ski mask and I couldn't make out his eyes. He was holding a gun, his stance practiced and correct, and he saw me peering around the doorway.

I saw him pull the trigger, and dodged back as sound of the shot rang out. I ran toward the door, my pulse throbbing wildly, and heard the man coming after me. I turned and saw him poised threateningly in my bedroom doorway. His eyes were dark and calm and he raised his gun again to shoot at me. Instinctively, I threw my vase at him and he misfired and swore.

I wasn't sure if the vase hit him or not, but I wasn't waiting around to see. I ran out the door and down the hallway, bursting through the fire escape door and racing down the stairs.

I don't think I'd ever moved so fast. My heart was pounding loudly, and the hairs on the back of my neck were still standing up. I raced down the first flight of stairs before I knew what I was doing, and then I dashed across the short landing and began to run down the next flight.

I heard the door to the stairwell bang open and a sudden rush of clarity flooded my body. I knew without turning back that the man in the mask was standing on the landing above, aiming his gun at me carefully. The stairwell was painted a brilliant white, and smelled vaguely of disinfect; the stairs were high and utilitarian. My mind was filled with a loud blankness and I took a few more stairs down, subconsciously readying myself to be shot.

There were six or seven more steps down to the landing, and at the last moment, I took a flying leap downwards. I landed on my feet, balancing in a half-crouch, and at the same moment I heard the shot ring out. The man had missed me because of my sudden leap, and I wasn't waiting to see if his next shot would hit its target.

Through a haze of terror and a dull thudding in my ears, I saw the red fire escape door. There was a handle – shiny steel, begging to be grabbed. The world seemed to have slowed down, and seconds were now as long as minutes. I watched as my hands moved of their own accord, my fingers wrapping around the cold steel. I pulled back with all my strength. It opened, and I slipped around to the other side. My ears rung with the noise of another shot – this time he'd managed to hit the fire escape door.

I lurched into the hallway and the door thudded closed behind me. I thought I heard steps – but maybe it was just my imagination. Either way, the man knew where I was and all he had to do was race down the stairs and open the door to see me.

The hallway was long and narrow, and I would be an easy target for him. I couldn't go back up the fire escape door, and other than the elevator, there was no way out of this floor.

I ran down the hallway, looking left and right for some place to hide, trying to figure out what to do next. There were no windows I could leap out of, no strategically placed alcoves I could hide in. I was almost at the end of the hallway when I saw an open door straight ahead. I barged in without thinking and slammed it behind me.

I found myself inside a condo, its door safely between me and the pursuer. An old man stood in the middle of the room, a bag of groceries under each arm, staring at me, agape. He was tall, with thick, straight white hair; he had turned around when he heard me slam his door and he didn't look too happy to see me.

I was panting heavily, and was most likely trembling from the shock; I was too terrified to notice. I put a finger against my lips and whispered, "Please let me hide here."

The man shook his head and placed his bags on the counter. "And why would I do that?"

I heard the heavy fire escape door slamming shut down the corridor, and then a man's deep voice called out softly. "Tee-fanny… I know you're down here somewhere…"

He sang it like a nursery rhyme and the softness of his voice made it all the more menacing. The old man and I both stared at each other in shock.

"Tee-fanny." The voice was louder now and I pressed my finger against my lips once more, pleading with the old man with my eyes.

"Where a-are yo-ou?"

I heard the man walk up the corridor and then back down. He called out, "I know you're hiding sooome wheeere."

I heard a door open down the hall and then an old woman's sharp, high-pitched scream. The door banged shut and the man swore loudly. His footsteps grew quieter as he started running away.

"Get away!" The woman screamed through her door. "Get away or I'm calling the cops!"

"I'm sorry!" I heard the man yell back. "It was a joke, I'm leaving!"

I heard the fire escape door slam shut once again and I peered through the spyhole. I couldn't see anyone out there and I breathed a loud sigh of relief.

The old man was looking at me curiously.

"It's ok," I told him, "I'm sorry about this."

His eyes were sharp and grey and they took in my sorry state. "You look like you could use a nice cup of tea," he announced, and I agreed with a nod.

I wanted to thank him for his help, but first I went and sat down on the sofa. I put my head between my knees, the way I'd learned in college, and stopped myself from fainting.

When I sat up a few minutes later, the man was putting teabags in two mugs and a kettle was boiling. "You like Earl Grey, don't you?" he asked and I nodded silently.

I was about to apologize for barging in, but then I noticed his massive grocery bags. "Wow," I said, "What're you doing with those gigantic bags of flour? And sugar, too."

He smiled at me. "Guess."

"Umm." I was bad at this game. "Are you going to bake something?"

"Bingo."

"What're you baking?"

I'd never met a man who baked before. I'd met men who barbequed, men who chopped vegetables, and even men who helped around the kitchen. But I'd never met a man who baked. I looked around the place – it was sparsely furnished and there were no flounces of feminine color. I was pretty sure he wasn't baking because of a nagging wife.

"I haven't decided yet," he said. "I used to be a pastry chef so now I bake things for fun."

My eyes widened. "You're a retired pastry chef?" I thought I might be dreaming. Maybe the aftermath of seeing the masked man in my apartment was making me hallucinate. "What do you bake, cakes and things?"

"Yes." He removed the teabags and handed me a mug. "I do cakes, muffins, cupcakes; the odd tart or pie… You know. Fun stuff."

I tried not to drool. "That does sound like fun." I took a better look at the man. He was definitely handsome, but definitely old. "Who eats all that stuff?"

He shrugged and took a sip of his tea. "I mostly give them away. I take them down to the Retirement Home and leave them there. Either I've been increasing the residents' diabetes, or the nurses are eating them."

"Wow. Lucky them." I stared at him wistfully. The man was handsome, he was nice, and he baked cupcakes. He was the perfect man for me. If only he'd been a couple of years younger… On the other hand, if he'd been a few years younger, I'd have professed my love for him right there and probably scared him off forever. My incredible passion would turn me into a crazed stalker. So maybe it was for the best that he was too old for me.

He smiled at me and brought an airtight box out of a cabinet. He opened it, found a plate and placed a cupcake on it. He passed the plate to me. "Try this."

I stared at the man and then down at the cupcake. It had white icing on top and I bit into it without hesitation. "Mmm... What is this, carrot?"

"Orange and poppyseed," he said, smiling. "I'm glad you like it."

"Like it? I love it! This is amazing." I made uncivilized noises and finished it up. "Mmm, thanks. That was so good."

The man was beaming happily and I felt a pang of guilt. "I'm really sorry about all this," I said, "I didn't mean to disrupt your day."

"Nonsense. This is nice. I don't get too much excitement here. It's rather a boring building, isn't it?"

"It is," I agreed. "What's your name?"

"Glenn Sterling," he said. "And I know you're T. Fanny."

I shook my head. "No. That's Tiffany. Tiffany Black."

"It's nice to meet you, Tiffany Black."

We smiled at each other and I said, "You know, if you need any help ever, umm, you know...Mixing stuff. Or moving furniture, or whatever. You can let me know. I'm sorry I barged in like this."

"No, really, that's fine. Although I may need someone to taste-test my new cake recipe."

I smiled happily. It was a strange way to make a new friend, but meeting Glenn almost made up for being shot at by that masked man. We beamed at each other and he gave me another cupcake. This time it was white chocolate and raspberry and almost as soon as it came into my grubby little hands, it was gone.

I was heavily sedated with tea and cupcakes, but I remembered to pull out my cell phone and call Stone.

"Yo," Stone answered.

"I need you to come to my place," I said, "But it's not very urgent. I've made a new friend and I'm going to wait for you in his apartment while we have cupcakes and tea."

Silence. And then, "Is that a euphemism? Did someone kidnap you?"

"No, I'm fine."

"But someone was waiting in your apartment?"

"Yeah."

"And you're safe now?"

"Yeah."

"I'll be there in ten."

He disconnected and I turned to Glen, who was watching me with a serious expression.

"If your ex-boyfriend's bothering you," he said, "You could call the cops. Get a restraining order."

I smiled, touched by his concern. "It's ok. I'm dealing with it."

He nodded. "Let me know if you ever my help. I might be seventy-nine, but I like to think that I could be helpful."

"You're seventy-nine? Wow. You're really handsome for an old guy."

I clapped my hands over my mouth but the words were already out. I had turned into Nanna.

Glen didn't seem to be offended. He laughed and said, "Thank you. It's nice to be appreciated for my looks instead of just my baking."

I laughed with him and thought again of Nanna. She could use a nice boyfriend like Glen, someone who was good-looking and interesting but not crazy. I said, "You're not seeing anyone, are you?"

As soon as the words were out, I realized I was setting up two people for my own greedy motives. In addition to turning into Nanna, I had also turned into my mom. I sighed. "I'm sorry. Forget I asked. You must have people setting you up all the time."

"Actually, I do," he said, "Men don't live as long as women, so us living guys are a bit in demand. I wish I'd been this popular when I was younger."

I smiled and wondered how I could introduce Nanna to him without being obvious about it.

My phone rang. "Hi, Stone," I said.

"What's the apartment number?"

"I'm in, umm." I pressed the phone against my shoulder and asked Glen, "What's your apartment number?"

"402B," he said, and I repeated it back to Stone.

He hung up and in two minutes, there was a knock on the door. I let him in and introduced him to Glen, before saying goodbye and promising to stop by to taste his new cake recipe soon.

We walked up the fire escape stairs to my level and Stone said, "Do you want to wait out here?"

I shook my head. I needed to see my apartment.

I walked with Stone to my door, and followed him across the threshold. I stood against one wall in the living room and surveyed the area. Stone had his gun in his hands, ready to shoot if required, and he prowled through my home, silent and deadly. I heard him opening the closet door, then the bathroom, and ruffling the curtains and clearing under the bed.

"No-one here," he called and I closed the door and bolted it shut with a sigh of relief. I hadn't expected there to be a second attacker lurking in the condo, but it was best to be on the safe side.

"What now?"

Stone surveyed the shattered remains of my ugly vase. "Did the guy break something?"

"No. I threw my vase at him."

He raised an eyebrow at me. I wanted to elaborate but I felt foolish in retrospect, treating my vase like a bullet, so I said nothing.

Stone said, "At least your Feng Shui's improved some. That vase was giving me the creeps."

I tried to think of something to say to defend my poor vase's honor, but I quickly gave up. He was right. The vase had been hideous and my place was better off without it.

Stone took my keys and locked and unlocked my door. "Guy's a good lock-pick," he said. "The lock works perfectly and you can't tell he broke in."

"Great," I said. "Should I buy another lock and hope he can't pick that one?"

Stone shook his head. "No point. Looks like he can pick just about anything."

"Wonderful. So now what?"

"I'd recommend you check into a casino for a few days until you sort this thing out."

I sighed. "You know you're meant to check into a hotel, right? Not a casino. Besides, I like living here."

"You can always tell Sophia you quit. I'm sure word'll get back to these guys."

"I can't quit. Word might not get back and then I'd be dead anyway. Plus, I actually found something out today."

Stone looked at me curiously but didn't say anything.

There was nothing to discuss. I headed into the bedroom and packed a bigger suitcase.

"If you check into the Treasury Casino," Stone said, "You won't have to travel to and from work."

"Only weirdoes live in the same place they work."

"I live where I work. The top floor's my apartment, the rest of the building's my office."

Me and my big mouth. "Not you, of course. I didn't mean you."

"No, of course not. How about you check in next door at the Tremonte? You can walk to and from work. Less weird?"

I nodded. "Definitely less weird."

"Good."

He walked me down to the parking lot and watched as I got into my car. "I'll meet you there," he said.

I parked my car in the Tremonte parking lot and headed to Reception. Stone was already there.

"How'd you get here before me?" I said. "I started driving before you."

"Valet parking, babe."

I imagined the snooty Tremonte valet sneering at my '99 Accord.

"I should check in," I said, and walked to the counter.

After I put down my credit card details and got my room key, Stone walked half-way to the elevators with me. "Be careful," he said. "Try to take a cab instead of driving. You can bill Sophia. And check your hotel room each time you enter. There are cameras all round the place, so I doubt anyone would try to break in, but it's better to be careful."

I nodded and watched him walk away.

I dumped my suitcase in my room, had a quick glance at the pretty view, packed my bag for work and headed out.

The bar I was meeting Emily at wasn't too crowded yet. It was only slightly off-Strip, but a bit too boring for the tourists. At this hour there were a few locals in, and I could tell there were at least five guys trying to work up the courage to ask Emily if they could buy her a drink.

Emily waved when she saw me. She looked great as usual – she had short, curly brown hair and beautiful green eyes.

We had met through mutual friends just over a year ago, and had quickly bonded over drinks, spa visits and trips to Vegas' mediocre art exhibitions. We spent a lot of time together, since most of our other friends were either married or engaged, while Emily was newly-divorced and I was just plain unlucky with men.

I liked her a lot, but we shared the kind of new friendship that was at once superficial, while also being deep and meaningful. Sometimes I wondered why she'd become a detective at the LVPD – she was clearly smart, sophisticated and ambitious, and would have done well in any career. Emily had moved here five years back with her husband, and I sensed there were things in her past she wasn't willing to share with me just yet.

"Thanks for meeting me," I said, as I slid into the chair opposite her. "It's been a while."

She nodded, and took a sip of her beer. "Yeah, I guess we both got busy. How're you doing?"

We exchanged a few details of our lives, and I ordered a martini and waited for the cocktail waitress to leave before I got down to business. I'd never asked Emily for a professional favor before, and I hoped this wouldn't change our friendship.

"I've got something to announce," I said. "You know how I'm always talking about leaving the casino gig and becoming a PI?"

"Ye-es…"

Emily looked at me warily and I went on, "Well, I've got my first case!"

"Hang on a second. Are you even accredited? Finished your training?"

I frowned. "My client doesn't care that I'm still in training."

"Ok. Who's your client?"

"Sophia Becker."

Emily let out a soft whistle. "And how's that going for you?"

"You don't think I'll uncover anything new?"

A guarded look came over Emily's face. She took her job as a law enforcement officer seriously, and I could tell she didn't think one of her colleagues could overlook anything, but she also didn't want to hurt my feelings by being too blunt.

"Sophia Becker," Emily started slowly, "May have hired you for many reasons. Not just to uncover something new. But maybe even just to be able to say during her trial that she hired a PI to uncover new evidence."

"You don't think she could be innocent?"

Emily shrugged. "It's not my job to decide who's innocent or not, it's not any Police Detective's job to do that. Our job is to find who the most likely suspect is. And at this stage, it's Sophia Becker."

"But – maybe it's not."

Emily sighed. "Look, off the record? This woman's as good as convicted. They found the gun in her bedroom, the one used to kill Ethan Becker. And she had motive, means and opportunity. There's not much else to look for."

"Can you tell me anything about the case?"

"No, 'fraid not. It wasn't my case anyway, so it's not like I'd know any details. But it's still an open case, which means I'm not allowed to say anything about it in public."

And like it or not, I was part of that public. My shoulders slumped and I twisted my lips. I didn't want to push Emily into revealing anything she wasn't meant to, but I still asked. "Can you at least give me the press release version?"

"Sure, why not? But I'm sure you've already read it in the press."

"I did, but maybe I missed something. Maybe just hearing you tell me will make me remember something."

Emily shrugged. "If you insist."

She repeated like a litany what I'd already read in the newspapers. Ethan Becker had been found dead in his car at 5am by a jogger, time of death was estimated at 1am; police had discovered the murder weapon in Sophia Becker's bedroom, she had been arrested as the chief suspect and was now out on a million-dollar bail.

It wasn't anything I didn't already know, but I still nodded, feeling that at least I'd tried my best. "What about Audrey Waldgraf?" I asked. "Do you know anything about that case?"

She looked at me, slightly puzzled. "That one's closed. Burglary gone wrong."

"Do you know who might have done it?"

"No." Emily shook her head. "We found prints, but they didn't match with anyone in the system, so it was someone who's never been arrested before."

"Hmm." I took a long sip of my martini. "Did you know Audrey was having an affair with Ethan Becker?"

Emily shook her head. "We heard rumors, but there was nothing conclusive."

"You don't think that's suspicious?"

"No. We couldn't prove they were having an affair. And even if they were, it doesn't mean anything."

"I don't know," I said. "I just find it too coincidental, don't you? Ethan's killed, then his supposed mistress dies?"

Emily looked down at her drink and then back at me. "I don't believe in coincidences, but this might just be one."

Talking about Audrey was reminding me of the guy who'd tried to kill me today. Before I could help myself, I said, "There was a guy in my condo today, waiting for me with a gun."

Emily looked at me in shock. "Are you sure he was *waiting* for you?"

I nodded. "And I'm pretty sure, if I hadn't run away in time, I'd be dead. Another 'burglary gone wrong' victim."

Emily looked at me carefully. "Are you ok? Hurt?"

"I'm fine. I just... I think this might've been how Audrey died."

Emily shook her head. "We don't know that. Do you know what he was after?"

"No, but I think it's got to do with the Ethan Becker investigation."

Emily sighed. "I wish I could offer you police protection or something, but you know the department's swamped. We've barely got enough resources to go after criminals…"

"It's ok." I reached out and squeezed her hand, touched by her concern. "I wasn't expecting special treatment. And besides, I'll be fine. I can take care of myself."

Hope glimmered in Emily's eyes. "You've been doing the self-defense training I was telling you about?"

"Uh, yeah. Absolutely. I've been taking classes." She didn't need to know it was only one so far.

"And you're getting yourself a gun?"

"Yep, applied for a permit and everything."

Emily leaned back in relief. "You know, I worry about you."

"You shouldn't. I can take care of myself."

Emily shook her head in exasperation and I changed the topic quickly, before she could give me a hard time about not being equipped to deal with the crazies. We chatted about a mutual friend who had gotten tired of Vegas and was moving to New York, and then Emily said, "You know, there's someone I've *got* to introduce you to. Drop by the precinct sometime. He's a new detective in Homicide, just transferred here from Miami."

"Ugh. You know how I hate set-ups."

"You won't hate this one."

I smiled at her and wondered if it was time to grow up and go on a blind date or two. It's not like I was getting any younger, and it's not like nice men were growing on trees. Or if they were, I hadn't yet discovered that tree.

"Ok," I said, "But make sure he knows just how fabulous I am. But don't talk me up too much."

Emily smiled. "I'll talk you up just the right amount."

I laughed, and we talked a bit about the latest blockbuster movie we were both looking forward to seeing. I promised Emily we'd make time to go watch it together, and after reassuring her that I'd take care of myself and keep going to my self-defense classes, I left and headed over to the Treasury, where I went through my nightly routine of pretending to be a friendly dealer.

CHAPTER SIXTEEN

It was convenient living next door to work and it was also nice to get back to my room after my shift and find it devoid of lock-picking, mask-wearing, gun-toting men. I was able to drift off quickly and I woke the next morning ready to tackle the world.

I had a quick breakfast at the buffet, skipping the eggs and hash browns and getting my morning serving of fruits from an apricot Danish and a blueberry muffin. I thought about Glen – if I was still living in my condo, maybe I could've headed downstairs and had breakfast with him. I wondered if he'd be willing to do a trade: he could supply breakfast pastries and I could supply – what, exactly? I racked my brains and tried to think of things I could barter for baked goods, but I couldn't come up with anything. The pleasure of my company would have to suffice.

Once I was back in my room, I connected to the casino wifi and logged into one of my social networking accounts.

A quick search for 'Audrey Waldgraf' brought up her profile and then it was just a matter of browsing through her list of friends, looking for someone who'd listed their phone number publicly.

Some of Audrey's friends didn't seem to care about their privacy at all. I was able to choose between no less than ten people and I finally picked a girl who had gone to college with Audrey. I figured she'd know.

She answered my call immediately. "Hello?"

"Amelia Murray?" I asked.

"Yes?"

She sounded like she was in her mid-twenties, slightly younger than me, but just young enough to be a whole lot more immature.

"Amelia, this is Caroline, one of Audrey Waldgraf's old friends. She gave me your number one time because we were out clubbing and we meant to invite you to join us."

"Oh my God, that's like, so sad. I'm so sorry about what happened to her and it's great that she wanted to hang out like that."

"Yeah, I know." I fake-commiserated and said, "So, I'm also trying to get in touch with her ex-boyfriend, but I don't have his phone number. Do you have it with you?"

"Derek? Yeah, I've got it, just a second."

Within a few minutes, I had Derek's phone number. I thanked Amelia for her help, told her we should hang out some time and hung up.

I called Derek's number and a confused-sounding guy said, "Oh. Yeah. Uh. elloHellfsdkjhfdjkfgHello."

I smiled brightly and put on my chipper voice. "Hi. Is that Derek?"

There was a pause and then a suspicious-sounding, "No-oo?"

"Who's that?"

"Nate?"

"Is Derek there?"

"No-oo."

"Is this his phone?"

"No-oo."

"Do you have Derek's phone number?"

"Ye-es."

"Could I have it please?"

"Oh. Kaay."

I'm not sure if I woke the guy up, if he was stoned or if he was in a bad mood. After he gave me Derek's phone number, I hung up and punched a fist in the air.

I called Derek's new number with some trepidation. For all I knew, Nate didn't really know Derek's number, or he'd made it up to mess with my head, or he was really Derek - pretending to be Nate.

It rang three times and someone picked up. "This is Derek."

"Derek." I breathed a sigh of relief and then the words came tumbling out. "Hi, I'm Tiffany Black, I'm a private investigator looking into Audrey's death. Is this a bad time for you?"

There was a long pause and then he said, "I'm sorry, who are you?"

"You're Audrey's ex-boyfriend, right?"

"Ye-es."

"I'm sorry to hear about her death. This must be very difficult for you, but I'm investigating what happened since I think the police might have missed something."

I could hear the wheels turning inside his head and then he said, "Ok."

"Ok! Well, would you like to have lunch with me today?"

"Where?"

"How about the McDonald's near Tremonte Casino?"

There was another pause as he pondered the option. "Ok."

I went back online and checked Amelia's social networking account again. There were two photos with a man tagged as Derek Girard and I tried to memorize the way he looked.

There were also a number of photos with a girl tagged as Audrey, and I looked at her carefully. She looked young and happy in the photos and she was cute in a way Sophia wasn't. Her cheeks were flushed and she had dark brown hair. I thought about the fact that her lock had been picked and that someone had also broken into my place. And I thought about Sophia's claim that someone had broken into her house and planted the gun. I thought the three events should be connected, but I couldn't see how.

I had two hours to kill before my lunch date, so I called the number for Max Desilva.

"This is Max," he answered, sounding vaguely sleepy.

I introduced myself and told him I was a PI investigating the Ethan Becker murder. "Would you mind if we had a chat sometime?"

"Not at all," he said, sounding friendlier than I'd expected. "What time works for you?"

I did the math: two hours from now I'd start lunch, and that should be over within an hour. "How about 3 pm?"

"Sounds alright. You wanna pick a place?"

I named a café that I knew was just a few minutes' walk from the McDonalds, and Max told me he'd meet me there. I was pleasantly surprised – I'd expected Max to be hostile and uncooperative, given his history with Ethan.

The last call I needed to make was to my parents. I had no idea if they'd left messages on my machine back in the condo, but I needed to at least let them know that I was staying in a hotel for a while.

When my mom picked up, I told her that I was staying at Tremonte for a few days while my condo was repainted. That was another white lie, and I refused to feel guilty about it.

Mom went silent for a few seconds after I told her about the repainting and I wondered whether she'd heard me ok. And then she said, "What's this really about? I know your condo's fine, why aren't you living there?" There was a brief pause and I tried to think of how to convince her that my condo really was being repainted. It was a terrible excuse and I should've thought of something better, but before I could say anything, Mom exclaimed, "I know! You've moved in with Stone! That's wonderful news."

My eyes widened and I said, "No Mom, I haven't moved in with Stone! He's just a friend! I wouldn't move in with him!"

"Give the phone to me," I heard Nanna say in the distance.

She must've snatched it away from my mom, and I heard her say, "Tiffany, you listen to me now." Her voice was bubbling over with enthusiasm and I stared blankly at the wall ahead of me. "Moving in with a man is a big step."

"I'm not moving in with anyone, Nanna. I've moved into a hotel for a few days."

She went on as though she hadn't heard me. "You don't buy the cow if you get the milk for free, but these days everyone lives together for a bit. It's the modern way of doing things. I'm not as old-fashioned as you think. Now, the important thing is to not look like a slob, like you usually do when you're home."

"I'm not mo-"

"Make sure you take some nice clothes to wear. Some lingerie, too. I know you don't own any of those Victoria's Secrets things men like these days, so you should go buy some. I can go with you if you want, help you pick out some nice stuff. I've got good taste in sexy things."

"I'm hanging up now," I said loudly. I love my Nanna, but I don't want to go lingerie-shopping with her. "I have to go out. Bye."

I stared down at my cellphone, wondering why Nanna didn't seem to be able to hear me when I said I wasn't living with Stone.

I must not have pressed the 'end call' button hard enough, because I heard Nanna's voice drifting out as she said to my mom, "Now isn't that wonderful news? Tiffany had to hang up. I guess she'd rather be with Stone now."

I groaned loudly and pressed the button, making sure the call was definitely over.

Derek was already at McDonald's when I arrived. He was hard to miss: tall, with thin, gaunt features.

I introduced myself and we went up to the counter to order. "It's my treat," I said, although it was really Sophia's treat, and I switched on the MP3 recording device hidden in my purse when I got out the money to pay.

We sat down with our meals and I watched as Derek gobbled up his massive burger in a few bites. Compared to him, I was a dainty eater, and I wondered how he didn't put on any weight.

"So," I said, in between bites. "I need to talk to you about Audrey."

Derek sighed heavily.

"You seem really depressed about the whole thing." I added.

"Yeah. I mean, you can't do anything if a burglar breaks in, but I wished she'd lived somewhere safer. Not in that old building."

I nodded. The idea of her death not being a burglary gone wrong didn't seem to have occurred to him. "You two were close, weren't you?"

He nodded and I felt as if I were prying food out of a lion's mouth. "Why'd you break up?"

He gobbled down a few more fries. "She outgrew me."

"How do you mean?" I glanced at his quickly depleting supply of fries. "I'm not hungry, would you like mine?"

He nodded and I passed them over, hoping my generosity would encourage some sharing. He munched on the fries and finally said, "I guess she grew up. We met in college, but I dropped out and got into the casino game, and she finished up and became a fancy accountant." He shrugged. "I wasn't good enough."

"But you stayed in touch."

"Sure."

"Did you try to get back with her?"

He looked at me. "What do you mean?" I shrugged and he narrowed his eyes and said, "Do you mean like, did I stalk her or break into her place or something? Because I didn't do any of that. She got involved with some casino hotshot where she was working, so I let it go. He was some rich dude, buying her diamond jewelry and taking her on weekend trips. I can't compete with that."

He sat brooding angrily and I said, "Do you know who the new boyfriend was?"

"No, I think she met him at work. He was older."

"Did she seem happy? Did she say anything about marrying him or being in love with him?"

"No. Hell no. She wouldn't marry him." He shook his head, probably more to convince himself than anything else. "She broke up with him, I think. Week before she died, I met her at friend's party and asked how her new boyfriend was. She said that was over."

"Did she say why it was over?"

"Nah. Just said she'd made a mistake."

We sat there, both lost in our own thoughts. After a while, I went up to the counter and got us each a slice of apple pie. It wasn't that great, but it was sweet, and it kept us sitting together.

I toyed with my slice to make it last longer. "Do you know anything at all about the new boyfriend?"

Derek looked at me with some curiosity. "Why? Think he might have something to do with the burglary?"

I shrugged. "I'm not sure. But nobody seems to know him."

Derek thought for a few moments and shook his head. "Audrey could be real secretive sometimes."

He finished his slice of pie all too soon. "I might as well get going. I need to get to my gig at El Toro."

El Toro was an old-school, run-down casino on the fringe of the Downtown district. It paid minimum wage and the gamblers there were stingy locals who never tipped. All dealers started out there, got a reference and some experience, and then moved to one of the bigger casinos if they were lucky, where players tipped and you could actually earn enough money to live off.

I fished about in my purse and handed him my card. "Call me if you think of anything."

He looked at it doubtfully. "Sure."

I didn't think he'd call me.

CHAPTER SEVENTEEN

I spent the time between appointments waiting at the café I'd chosen. It was a quiet, semi-dark place and there were few patrons at that hour. Other than three skinny men who looked like unemployed scriptwriters, I was the only customer, and I settled at a corner table.

Escaping from the shooter had given me a greater appreciation for my privacy and safety, and I couldn't help but think that Stone's idea of moving into the Tremonte had been brilliant. I smiled to myself, imagining someone wearing a black ski-mask waiting for me in my empty apartment for hours and hours. Hopefully, they would get a cramp.

I fished my MP3 player out of my bag, attached my headphones, and replayed my conversation with Derek. I felt like I was missing something; I tried to use his words to piece together a link between Ethan and Audrey's deaths.

If their affair was a secret, there were very few people who knew they could be connected. Sophia was one and Derek was another – but perhaps he'd lied about the whole thing; perhaps he was the one who'd killed Ethan and then he'd gone after Audrey when she'd refused to come back to him. All I needed was some way to prove that Ethan knew Derek, and would have pulled over to the side of the road for him.

On the other hand, perhaps I was looking at the whole thing from the wrong angle. I tried to forget about Derek and think about everyone else I'd talked to. As the minutes ticked by, I grew more and more frustrated. I knew I was missing something right in front of my eyes. I searched desperately for what it might be, but nothing jumped out at me, and the minutes slid by as if they were seconds, and before I knew it, it was time for my meeting with Max.

I recognized Max as soon as he walked into the café. He was short, stout and balding, and he beamed at the world in general.

I smiled and waved at him as he walked over with a spring in his step. I couldn't imagine him even being mildly irritated, let alone angry enough to yell at someone.

We introduced ourselves and I thanked him for coming at such short notice.

"No problem," he said, "I have lots of free time."

He looked as though he did, but I kept that thought to myself. I couldn't imagine someone having a job and still looking so relaxed, unless they were on holiday.

"I heard you used to be manager of the Riverbelle," I said and he laughed.

"Oh, yes, I can't believe those times. Feels like a lifetime ago."

"I thought you didn't want to leave?"

"No. That was just me being short-sighted. I wasn't happy to leave at first, but then I got a fabulous consulting position with the Riviera. And now look at me! Great pay, lots of free time and fun work, once in a while."

"Sounds impressive. So things worked out for you?"

"Oh, absolutely."

The waitress arrived with Max's coffee and he graced her with another cheerful smile. If he hadn't been so likeable, his joyful demeanor would have been annoying.

When the waitress left, I said, "Why were you so angry when you left the Riverbelle?"

Max looked at me seriously, his sunny disposition clouding over momentarily. "I didn't leave, I was forced to resign."

"Why?"

"They wanted to promote Steven Macarthur. He was an up-and-comer and a hard-worker, not an old lazy-bones like me."

"That doesn't sound unreasonable." I smiled. "Everyone wants employees to work hard for them."

Max nodded. "I guess you're right. But I was worried I wouldn't get a new job at my age."

"But it happened."

"Yes. Steven set up an interview with a friend of his."

"That was nice of him."

Max leaned back in his chair and crossed his arms. He narrowed his eyes and hunched his shoulders. "Sure, it was nice of him."

He looked like a completely different man and I tried to hide my surprise. Obviously he was hiding something and I tried to think fast. He wasn't telling me the real reason why Steven had given him his job. I didn't know why this was important, or why he would bother to try and hide it, but the lie bothered me. If Steven didn't like Max, there were only a few reasons why he'd help him out. Either he felt sorry for Max, or Max had convinced him, somehow.

"You know," I said, "Steven didn't seem like a very nice man to me. Why'd he really get you the job?"

Max shrugged. "I guess even the meanest people have some niceness about them."

"Or maybe you bribed him. I'm sure the Riviera wouldn't like knowing that."

"I didn't bribe him."

"Then maybe you blackmailed him."

Max's eyes widened slightly and I knew I'd struck a nerve. "Come on, Max," I pleaded, "What difference does it make now, after all this time? Neither of us likes Steven and if you've got some dirt on him, it would really help my investigation."

He frowned and shook his head. "Nobody's meant to know this."

"But I already do. If you don't tell me know, you know I'll just go to Steven and try to get it out of him."

Max sighed and I could see I was wearing down his defenses.

"Please," I said, "please, please, pretty please? You can see I'm desperate!"

He sighed again and his lips tightened into a thin smile. "Fine," he said, looking almost like his old self again, "But if you tell anyone this, I'll deny it."

"Scouts' honor," I said, holding up three fingers even though I'd only ever been in the Brownies for a week.

Max leaned forward. "You have to understand. I was desperate. I had expenses and a lifestyle I'd gotten used to." He took a sip of coffee and went on. "I've never liked Steven. He's too smarmy for his own good; comes into work too early and kisses ass too much. I blame him for pushing me out of my job. So after I got fired, I followed him home for a couple of days."

"What did you see?"

"He was having drinks with a group of dealers and security guys."

"That doesn't sound too bad."

"No. But after I saw them together, I visited the casino floor a few times." He paused and looked at me. "Do you know why casinos have so many security guys?"

"To make sure players don't cause trouble?"

"And to make sure dealers don't cause trouble."

My jaw almost dropped to the floor, I knew exactly what he was about to say. "Oh no."

"Oh yes. I didn't have proof, but I had enough to scare him."

"So you never reported him…"

Max gulped. "Look, if I had proof, I would've told Ethan or Neil. But I didn't have any proof and Ethan wasn't talking to me."

"How'd he do it?"

"I'm not sure."

"But you must have a good hunch."

"Well…" He looked at me carefully, and I guess he decided I could be trusted. "I think one of the dealers swiped a pack of chips each time the guards came by for collection. All Steven had to do was not report them."

I sat in silence, completely awed. It was the Big One, the one all the jackpot-chasers were after. Except it wasn't a jackpot. It was the mother lode of all scams, one that was untraceable because it was run by the guys on the inside.

"This is big," I said.

"It's huge," he agreed. "But I had no proof. Just enough of a suspicion to threaten him."

"Steven doesn't seem like a nice person," I mused. "But he's never been a suspect in Ethan's murder. The guy's got the perfect alibi."

"Even if he had no alibi, I'd never believe he'd kill Ethan."

"Why not?"

"He'd never hurt the guy. He had everything arranged perfectly for himself and he had Ethan eating right out of his hand. He'd never mess that up."

That made sense. I'd only met Steven very briefly but he'd seemed smart and focused, unlikely to do anything stupid. "You don't like Steven," I said. It was more of a statement than a question, and Max smiled.

"No, I don't. What else did you want to ask me?"

"What's Thelma Durant like?"

He shrugged. "Nice enough. Doesn't come into the office too often. Prefers to head to the spa."

"And her husband?"

"Does a lot of work at the casino. Nice guy. The women all love him." He winked at me and I tried my best not to giggle.

"Did he get along with Ethan?"

Max took another sip of his coffee. "They argued a bit. Ethan wasn't too thrilled about Neil at first, but I think he respected the man after a few years."

"Leo?"

"He was pretty young when I was working there."

"Sophia?"

He shook his head. "I'm still surprised at that marriage. You know, everyone thought she was a scheming gold-digger. And now she's proven them all right."

I sighed. "She hired me, you know."

"Doesn't mean a thing. It's just to look good in front of the jury later on."

I was tired of hearing that line. I didn't want to believe it. I was feeling annoyed and I said, "I went to the Riverbelle to talk to the guys there. And you know what happened? Some thugs tried to back-room me."

Max looked at me in surprise. "They still have that room there?"

"You knew about it?"

He shook his head. "We had that room there for emergencies, even though we never used it. Everyone at the casino knew about it."

I sighed. It was just as I'd feared. Too many people had access to the place and anyone at the casino could've hired Beady Eyes and Mr. Beard to threaten me.

Our coffees were finished and I said, "I'll call you if I think of anything else. And here's my card. Let me know if you think of something."

"I will," he said, pocketing my card.

CHAPTER EIGHTEEN

When I got back to the Tremonte, I called Thelma. She was the one person I hadn't talked to yet and, though I didn't think she would be any help, I needed to contact her.

She answered after about five rings. When I introduced myself, she went quiet for a moment and then said, "Who are you working for?"

"Sophia Becker."

She snorted. "Good luck with that."

I could tell she was about to hang up, so I interjected quickly. "The investigation could uncover who really killed Ethan."

"We all know it was Sophia."

"I've discovered some things the police overlooked. I'd really appreciate your help."

"And what if you find more evidence that it was Sophia?"

"I'll go to the police with it." The truth was I didn't want to believe I'd find more evidence damning Sophia.

"I'm busy," she said. "Can we just do this over the phone?"

"I'm afraid not." The one thing I'd learned during my training was that people were more forthcoming face-to-face. "I could meet you anywhere you'd like, a café or a restaurant or your house."

"Ok. You can come over to my house the day after tomorrow."

It was a victory of sorts but I still said, "Are you free any time before that?"

"No. I'm busy."

She hung up and I heard the line go dead. I stared at my phone and put it away with a wry look. She hadn't told me what time to go over, so I'd need to call her again tomorrow to check. For all I knew, she didn't actually intend to meet me.

I called Leo next. I introduced myself when he answered and hoped he'd remember me.

He did. He said, "Oh hey, what were you doing in the casino that day?"

"I went by to talk to your Uncle Neil. What were you doing?"

"My aunt told me she'd give me a tour and she did. It's a massive place and it was nice to see where Dad worked. I think maybe I'll go work there once I've finished school."

"Thelma must've been happy to hear that."

He made a non-committal noise and said, "I'm not sure. She wanted me to sell her my shares of the casino, but I'd rather not. I said that if Sophia lost the case, we could divvy up Sophia's shares instead of me getting them all, but we'll see. I don't want to argue about the casino with her."

I wondered if Leo was heading into a legal minefield. If Thelma was serious about getting control of the casino, she might not give up so easily.

I asked Leo what he thought of Steven Macarthur, but he didn't have much of an opinion. So after chatting about the weather for a bit – we both wished it would just cool down already – I told me to call him if he ever needed to chat and hung up.

The next person I needed to talk to was Neil Durant. I called his cell phone and thought I detected a hint of annoyance when he answered.

"Neil, it's me, Tiffany."

"Pleasure to hear from you," he said, his tone of voice implying that it was anything but a pleasure.

"I have a favor to ask."

"Yes?"

"I wonder if Ethan might have known a young guy, Derek Girard?"

"Name doesn't ring a bell. Why?"

"Um, it's hard to explain, but I think he might be connected somehow. He's works at one of the Downtown casinos, and I thought he might have worked at the Riverbelle, maybe."

"Hmm."

"Do you think you could look into it? I'd really appreciate it."

He let out a short, exasperated sigh and said, "Sure, why not. I'll tell HR to run a profile."

"Great." An idea occurred to me and I said, "Do you think we could meet up after work today?"

He was instantly suspicious. "Why? I have somewhere I need to be."

"It'll be just two minutes. I have some information that might be useful to you."

"Like what?'

"Just meet me, ok?" I gave him the name of a quiet diner. "When can you be there?"

"An hour from now."

We hung up and I gave myself a virtual pat on the back. I didn't know if this would go anywhere, but it was worth a shot. I had the feeling that almost everyone I talked to was hiding something from me, and my chat with Max had given me a brilliant idea.

I drove to the diner, arriving a few minutes early and enjoyed a delicious apple cobbler as I waited for Neil to arrive. The place served Southern-style comfort foods and I figured I might as well eat while I was there.

Neil arrived a few minutes late, which meant that my cobbler had a good few bites into it. I'd already paid for it at the counter, and when Neil sat down opposite me, I offered him a bite.

"No thanks," he said. "I talked to HR about Derek."

I put down my fork. "And?"

"Derek applied for work at the Riverbelle but was turned down because his interview didn't go that great. We told him he could reapply once he'd gotten a bit more experience."

"Was Ethan at the interview?"

Neil looked at me like I was stupid. "No, of course not. That was a dealer interview, the HR guys take care of it."

I did feel a bit naïve, but how was I supposed to know which interviews a CEO deems worthy of his time?

"What did you want to talk to me about?" Neil said.

I swallowed a bit of cobbler quickly. "I heard a rumor there might be a ring of dealers stealing chips."

Neil's eyes narrowed. "Where did you hear that?"

I shrugged. "Can't name sources. But I guess you could look into your surveillance. Besides, some of your security guys are thugs. Do you know two of them threatened me the other day I was there?"

Neil smiled. "Were you trying to beat up another player?"

"I wasn't even in the pit! This wasn't about gambling. They told me to stay off the case."

Neil looked at me seriously and shook his head. "I don't know what you're talking about. And if we're done here, I have to get going."

I watched him head out the door and I quickly wolfed down another mouthful of cobbler before following him into the parking lot. I started up my car and followed his large black SUV toward the expressway. I figured he was heading towards his house at Lake Las Vegas. He picked up speed once we hit the expressway, but I kept an eye on him. When he signaled that he was exiting, I was only two cars behind him and I followed him onto Lake Mead

Parkway. I expected him to keep going till he got to his gated community, but he surprised me after two minutes by taking a quick right.

We both drove at a slower pace along less busy suburban streets; he didn't seem to have seen me and I followed him as he took left and right turns in quick succession. He parked on the side of the street and I quickly pulled into an empty driveway, crossing my fingers that the homeowners were out. Nobody seemed to have noticed me and I cut my engine and watched as he walked up to a modest house. He knocked, the door opened, and he disappeared inside.

I figured he would be at least a few minutes, so I moved out of the driveway before someone complained and parked right behind his SUV.

The minutes crawled by and became hours, and I watched as the sky grew darker and the sun set. Lights began to go on in the nearby houses and I imagined that dinner was being served. I regretted not bringing something to eat with me. Although I'd eaten up that large slice of cobbler in the diner, it clearly wasn't enough sustenance for a stakeout.

Just when I was wondering if Neil had stepped into a black hole, the lights went on inside the house he'd disappeared inside. I watched as the front door opened and Neil stepped outside. He leaned back inside and kissed someone. When he stepped away and began walking towards the street, I caught a glimpse of long, bare legs and blonde hair before the door closed.

When he was two feet from his car, I stepped out of mine.

Neil's eyes grew saucer-like and he stared at me for a long minute without blinking.

"I,Hi,Hi," I said. "Remember me?"

He finally found his tongue and shook his head as if to clear the disbelief from his mind. "What do you want? Are you here to blackmail me?"

"Why would I blackmail you? I'm a nice girl and honestly, I'm a bit hurt by the accusation."

"Then why are you here?"

"I just wanted to talk to you. But now I see why you were in such a rush to leave the diner. She must be really special if you gave up eating the world's best apple cobbler for her. How does Thelma feel about her?"

He scowled. "Leave Thelma out of this."

I stepped forward, feeling like I'd just been hit with a thunderbolt. "I get it now. No wonder you were two hours late getting home the night Ethan was murdered! You did leave when you said and you did take a detour."

His scowl deepened. "So what if I did?"

"You had a great alibi but you couldn't use it because then your wife would have grounds for divorce, and you'd lose everything you've gotten used to."

He shrugged. "What's that got to do with anything?"

"That gun in Sophia's bedroom was convenient."

We stared at each other for a while longer.

Finally, Neil said, "You wouldn't tell Thelma, would you?"

I shook my head, no. "So nobody else knows about this woman?"

"Ethan found out, but he kept my secret and I kept his."

"You knew about Audrey? Why didn't you tell me earlier?"

"No." He blinked in surprise. "He never had anything with Audrey. Ethan knew to stay away from co-workers. He was seeing Vanessa, his ex-wife."

CHAPTER NINETEEN

My heart almost stopped and I froze in place. Vanessa. I thought back to the slim, elegant woman and wondered why she'd be with Ethan.

"Are you sure?" I asked slowly, but I already knew the answer.

"Of course I'm sure. And I told Ethan I knew. That's the only reason he didn't tell Thelma about my girlfriend."

I sighed. "Why can't you guys just stick to one woman?"

Neil shrugged, got into his car and drove away.

I woke up early the next morning feeling strangely exuberant and optimistic. Maybe Max's cheerfulness had rubbed off on me, but I felt as though life were good.

I wasn't brave enough to re-enter the Riverbelle, because I still didn't know who had hired Mr. Beard and Beady Eyes. But I did want to have a conversation with Steven. If Max had managed to blackmail the man into

171

giving him a job, maybe I could blackmail Steven into talking to me. Of course, Steven was manager now, and maybe he'd cleaned up his act and I'd have nothing on him. Still, it was worth a shot.

I called Vanessa. It was only eight, but she answered the phone with the annoying alertness that morning people have.

"Vanessa, it's me, Tiffany," I said, "Do you mind if I come over to talk to you? Something's come up."

"Can it wait?"

She sounded doubtful, so I decided to fib a little. Living at the Tremonte was nice, but I was eager to go back to my old, boring condo.

"It's about Sophia," I said, "And I thought you might be able to help."

"Ok," she said. I told her I'd swing by in an hour.

I rushed to get dressed and was just applying mascara when my phone buzzed. I paused mid-swipe, and checked the caller ID. Stone.

I finished applying my mascara and called him back. "Hey Stone, what's up?"

"Checking in. Everything ok at the Tremonte?"

"It's all good," I said, "My room's intruder-free and I've been sleeping well at night. I don't think they've figured out I'm living here, whoever they are."

"You driving?"

"Umm. I took a cab a few times. I drove yesterday and there didn't seem to be anyone following me."

There was a pause and then he asked, "How do you know?"

I shrugged. "Just that feeling."

He took some time to think about it and then he said, "Take a cab. From now on. Until we find out who is following you."

I felt a brief moment of panic. Why was Stone acting so worried? "Is anything wrong?"

"Your gun license should've been here already. They're being slow. I want you to be extra-careful till I know you're packing."

"Fine." I sighed. Who would've known I'd miss my beat-up Accord and tiny condo so much?

"Where're you going today?"

I wondered if I should try to keep secrets from Stone. I hardly knew the guy and Sophia had hired him. I frowned, wondering if this was all a grand scheme of hers – hire a detective to look good in court, then hire someone to kill said detective before she found out too much. I mentally shook myself. No, that couldn't be true.

I decided to trust Stone. "I'm talking to Vanessa Conigliani at her Summerlin house in a few minutes. I guess I'll head back to the Strip after that and maybe try to talk to some other people."

"Ok." There was a pause. "Call me if you need me."

He hung up abruptly. I wondered if he even knew how to make small talk.

The cab dropped me off in front of Vanessa's house and as soon as I rang the bell she opened the door.

She was looking as beautiful as ever. She wore minimal makeup and another gorgeous silk print top with white capri pants. She wore no jewelry and there was something delicate and attractive about her.

"What happened to your car?" she asked and I made a face.

"Long story, don't ask." I headed into the living room and sat down.

Vanessa sat opposite me and asked, "What's going on?"

I looked at her carefully. She seemed smooth and unruffled, like one of those people who always had their life under control.

"Ethan Becker," I said. "Tell me about him."

She shrugged. "I already told you. I fell for him when I was too young to know better, we got married and then we got divorced."

"You wasted precious years of your life with him."

"Yes." She looked annoyed at having been reminded. "I already told you this. I regret having married him."

"Then why did you take him back? I know you were having an affair with him."

She looked at me in surprise and then she nodded. "So you found out."

"Yes. What was that about?"

She sat silently. I decided to give it a shot, sound out my theory. "You hated that he left you," I said. "You always thought things might've worked out, that you could've had a marriage that worked. But he refused to see it that way and he stiffed you in the divorce. You told yourself he wasn't the marriage type, but two years ago he married some two-bit stripper and you wanted to die of jealousy. It must've been hard seeing him marry that floozy."

Vanessa narrowed her eyes. "You know Sophia better than I do."

I nodded. "She isn't wife material."

"Exactly. Anyway, why bring all this up now?"

"You decided to steal him away from her."

She laughed shortly. "There were always women trying to 'steal him away.'"

"But you didn't even have to try. He fell for you. Who wouldn't?"

She smiled a tiny, flattered smile and I could see her struggle with her emotions. She had kept the secret for so long; it was prudent not to tell anyone. And yet, at the same time, the weight of keeping the secret was bearing down on her. She needed to get it off her chest. She needed to tell someone, anyone. A no-body like me, someone who wasn't a part of her social circle, would be perfect. And yet – secrets were always safer when they were kept.

In the end, the need to unburden herself won out. "He fell like a ton of bricks," she said, smiling at the memory. "And for once, I played my cards well. He had to chase me. He had to buy me nice things - dinners and holidays and gifts. I didn't care about those things, but it was nice to see him work for it. And he told me he loved me, that he wanted to be happy with me."

"What went wrong?"

She frowned and shook her head. "I don't want to talk about it."

"Let me guess. He said he didn't really love you. He wanted to make things work with Sophia and he was ready to get therapy."

"He was supposed to try to make things work with me."

"So you snapped. He'd rejected you once and he was rejecting you again, and you couldn't handle it. What did you do, ask him to give you a lift and then make him pull over when you had a fight? You killed him, didn't you?"

She stared into space blankly, her eyes not seeing me. She murmured, "It was all so sudden."

And then she snapped back to reality and her eyes focused on me.

"You killed him," I said. "And then you found out when Sophia wouldn't be home and entered her house with the key Ethan had given you. You put the gun in her nightstand and gave the police an anonymous tip. The perfect revenge."

I could see that Vanessa was determined not to say anything more, so I continued, "And then you tracked down Audrey and killed her."

She snapped back to reality and frowned and shook her head. "I don't know what you're talking about. I don't know any Audrey."

"It's ok," I said, "It doesn't make a difference. How did you break into her place?"

Her frown grew deeper. "Who's Audrey?"

"You know who she is. How did you break into her apartment?"

"I didn't. I don't know what you mean."

"You hired someone to break into my place, too. And you hired someone to follow me around."

She shook her head again. "I have no idea what you're saying. And I wouldn't bother to hire anyone to threaten you."

"Oh, come on. There's no point denying it now."

It annoyed me a little that Vanessa confided in me and told me everything – but then refused to admit to killing Audrey. I thought about a masked man waiting for Audrey in her darkened apartment, and the image bothered me. How did Vanessa, the ultimate sophisticate, tie in with that image?

I looked at Vanessa expectantly, but she was frowning at me and didn't say anything, so I stood up to leave. Just then, Vanessa stood up too, and said, "Wait. I need to show you something."

I thought she would tell me something about Audrey, maybe show me pictures of her, so I waited expectantly as she walked over to a large, wide-mouthed ceramic vase. She reached in, and I wondered what she could possibly keep inside it. Something secret, obviously. Maybe something valuable. It seemed like a great hiding place for something no-body else should know about, something like –

Vanessa pulled out her hand. She was holding a gun and the barrel was pointed right at me. I took a step back.

"Don't move," Vanessa said.

How could I have been so stupid as to expect her to pull out photos of Audrey from a vase? I mentally slapped my forehead and wondered what to do. I could try to make a run for it, but she looked ready to pull the trigger at any moment. "You don't mean this," I said slowly. "You don't want to shoot me. You got mad and shot Ethan, but it wasn't intentional. The police will understand."

Vanessa shook her head. "I can't have you blabbing to Sophia about this. I didn't mean to kill Ethan, but then the whole thing got tied up so nicely. I can't let you untie it now."

My heart was racing now and everything around me seemed to fade away into insignificance. All I could see was that large barrel. Any moment a bullet could come whizzing out and shoot me. I couldn't let that happen, not when my life was finally starting to pick up. I'd just met Glen and I was looking forward to having more of his cupcakes. Nanna was becoming a better poker player and someday she'd go on to win the World Series of Poker and then she'd thank me on live TV. Emily had promised to introduce me to a cute guy and if I could just get out of this alive, I could prevent Sophia from being convicted of murder.

"I'll do whatever you want," I said, "Just don't shoot me."

"Good." She seemed to relax a bit. "I'm glad you're being logical."

She walked towards the wall, moving sideways, keeping the gun trained on me. She opened a door I'd seen earlier, and moved away a bit.

"In there," she said and I obliged, moving slowly toward the door, trying to figure out how I could escape.

The door opened into the garage and I could see her large silver SUV sitting there. I heard a clicking noise; she'd unlocked the car.

"Get in," she said.

I glanced around, wondering if there was any way I could get out of here. But the garage was locked, its automatic roller door preventing any escape and, behind me, Vanessa was standing in the way with her gun.

I opened the door and climbed into the elevated passenger seat wordlessly. I wondered if I could try to call Stone. Maybe I could pretend to be looking for my sunglasses in my bag, and surreptitiously press a few buttons.

Vanessa walked around to the other side and got into the driver's side, her gun still pointed at me. She was watching me carefully and said, "Put both hands behind your head. I don't want you to try anything funny."

I cursed silently and did as she said. The plan to call for help vaporized into thin air. I closed my eyes and breathed, trying to keep calm and hoping I'd think of something else. I heard Vanessa buckle her seatbelt and then I heard the garage door opening.

When I opened my eyes Vanessa had slid the car out of the garage and we were moving down the street. She had one hand on the steering wheel, the other hand held the gun, keeping it low and pointed at me. She drove rapidly through the suburban streets, weaving and picking up speed as we merged onto the Las Vegas Beltway.

I heard a strangled noise escape from my throat. She could get us both killed by driving like a madman with only one hand on the wheel. A car swerved and its driver honked at us angrily and I groaned.

"Can't you drive more carefully?" I said.

"My driving's fine."

"That's what they all say!"

She didn't say anything in reply, so I tried to calm her down. "Killing me won't solve anything," I said. "I know you think you'll get away with it, but there are people who know where I went." She didn't look impressed so I fibbed, "I'm meant to meet my boyfriend in a few hours' time."

"What's your boyfriend's name?"

She had me stumped. I paused for a moment and said the first name that came to my mind. "Stone."

Vanessa laughed. "That's not a real name."

I kicked myself. For my next case, I'd have a slew of excuses and names and fake dates all lined up.

But for now, I needed to get out of here. Vanessa took the Durango Drive exit and a few minutes later we were driving down Pahrump Valley, the high desert mountains rising up on both sides of the road. The air inside the car was still and my blood was starting to run cold.

The road was almost empty at this time of the day, and the desert mountains on either side of the tarmac looked isolated and pristine. We passed a minivan, with a family of tourists, which had pulled over on the side of the road. The middle-aged driver stood with his arms around his young son and daughter while his wife took a photo of them. *A day out in the Nevada desert,* I thought bitterly.

The road grew emptier as we drove further into the desert, and it began to feel like we were miles from civilization. I opened my mouth once to speak, but before I could utter a word, Vanessa cut me off sharply. "Be quiet."

I sat silently for a few minutes and then I tried again. "The police will figure it out. There's no real benefit to killing me."

"I said, be quiet."

My heart thudded loudly and I wondered who would miss me. When would they find my body? It was sad and strange to know I was going to die soon. It felt unreal, as though this whole thing was a big joke. Like when they kidnapped guys during their bachelor party. I tried to tell myself that it was all just a good natured joke, but I was failing miserably.

Vanessa pulled over sharply on the side of the road. She opened her door, jumped out, and stood there, pointing the gun at me through the open door.

"Get out," she said.

I shook my head. "No. You won't kill me as long as I'm sitting in this car."

"Do you really want to test me?"

I thought of Ethan Becker, sitting there at the side of the road. Vanessa had shot one person in a car, and she probably didn't need to shoot another. I sighed and opened the door.

"And bring your purse," she called.

I picked up my heavy tote and stepped out regretfully. I looked around, but I couldn't see any other cars. The road stretched on for miles and there would be no point in trying to make a dash for it. Where would I even run to? Vanessa could see me clearly and she'd just shoot.

Vanessa's gun was trained on me and I wondered if it would've helped if my gun license had come through. I could have had a gun with me and then maybe the two of us could've gotten into a duel. I thought sadly of Stone and wondered if my death would make him sad. It might, but probably not as sad as it would make me.

"Walk up the hill, away from the road."

Vanessa's voice was calm and I smiled at her. "Making it hard for them to find my dead body?"

I was trying to be helpful, but Vanessa didn't even react. I climbed slowly. Every step was a step closer to my grave and I didn't want to rush things.

I heard Vanessa walking up behind me and I glanced back.

"Hurry up," she said, "I haven't got all day."

"I wish you did," I joked back, but she didn't laugh. The woman clearly had no sense of humor.

I thought I heard a noise, and I looked to the right. In the far distance, I saw a car approaching. Vanessa heard it too, and she glanced in the same direction.

"Hurry up," she said again, "If you don't walk faster I'll have to shoot you in the leg."

"How would that help me walk faster?"

I turned around and watched her come closer to me. Obviously she was worried that the driver of the car would see us, but I doubted it. People rarely notice what's going on around them and anyone who saw us would probably just assume we were two crazy tourists. Vanessa pulled her gun closer to her body, all the better for the driver to not see it. She stood a few feet behind me and said, "Come on. I need you to walk faster."

I turned around to look at her. And then before I could think, I threw my bag violently at her face.

She ducked, surprised, and I lunged at her. I fell on top of her heavily and she moved her arm, trying to angle the gun at me. I moved upwards, grabbed her hand and then banged the gun against the ground. Vanessa yelped in pain as her hand hit a rock.

"Let go!" I screeched. "Let go of the gun!"

But she wouldn't let go and as she lay under me on the ground, I felt her kick me and try to push me off. But she was a slim fifty-something-year-old, and my extra weight was coming in useful for once as I pinned her down. I tried to focus, and she kneed me in the stomach.

I grunted, and then I pressed down her finger, forcing her to pull the trigger. The gun went off once, twice, and I kept pulling until no more shots rang out. I figured it was safe to let go, so I moved my hand away and pressed down on Vanessa's shoulders to hold her down.

"Stop kicking me," I said.

I heard a noise and then a shadow fell across us. I looked up.

Stone was standing beside us, the gun in his hand pointed downward. For the second time since I'd met him, I saw the glimmer of a smile on his angular face.

"This is unexpected," he said.

CHAPTER TWENTY

I watched Vanessa go pale.

"Can I get up?" I said.

"Yes."

A wave of relief washed through me and I wondered if I could hug Stone. Probably not. There was that gun in his hand, and more importantly, he seemed to value his personal space.

I stood up quickly and said, "How did you find me?"

"Put a tracker on your phone when we went to your parents'."

"You *what?*" I stared at him in disbelief and my anger bubbled up. This man had no limits on invading my privacy. First he went through my phone book and then he attached a tracker. Of course, it had come in useful. But that wasn't the point.

"You told me you'd come back after talking to Vanessa," he said, "But I saw you heading into the desert. No-one goes into the desert unless they're a tourist."

I looked down and saw his car parked behind Vanessa's SUV. She was getting up slowly and I noticed her hand was bleeding.

"Sorry about that," I told her. "But you were trying to kill me."

Stone pulled a pair of handcuffs from his pocket and handed them to me. He didn't say anything. I snapped the cuffs on Vanessa and we all headed back down to the cars. I carried Vanessa's gun gingerly in my hand. I knew it was empty but I still didn't want to carry it.

Vanessa sat in her SUV while Stone called the police and we waited for them to arrive. I couldn't hear his conversation, but a trooper pulled up within a few minutes and two officers got out – a tall, broad man with dark brown hair and a stern expression, and a brunette who looked pretty enough to be a model.

"Stone," the stern-looking man said. "Good to see you again."

The two did a ritualistic hand thing, and then he introduced his partner. "This is Detective O'Hara." He looked at me. "I'm Detective Steve Costaki."

"Tiffany Black," I said, and we shook hands.

Detective O'Hara escorted Vanessa to the trooper, and Detective Costaki said, "We'll see you two at the station?"

Stone nodded silently, and the trooper drove off. I made sure Vanessa's SUV was locked up properly. It was a pretty car and it was a shame to leave it lying there, but I knew the police would come back for it.

Stone and I drove to the police station, where we waited for a while and then gave separate statements. I told officer interviewing me that Vanessa had confessed to killing Ethan Becker.

I had been thinking about it during my ride to the station. "You should check taxi records. I'm sure she called for a taxi soon after Mr. Becker's death, from some place nearby."

The officer taking my statement nodded and made a note and I hoped they'd follow it up.

When I finished giving my statement, I saw that Stone was still giving his. I sent Emily a text to let her know I was at the precinct and she came over within minutes.

"I heard all about it," she said, giving me a quick hug. "Let's get some coffee while we wait for Stone."

She herded me into the staff kitchen and poured me a cup of coffee. There was another detective in the room and Emily introduced us. "Tiff, this is Detective Nick Carlton. He transferred here from Miami."

"Hi," I said, smiling slightly.

Nick was tall and slender and wore a dark shirt with the sleeves rolled up. He skin was tanned, his hair was a dark crew cut and his eyes were a warm chocolate brown. He smiled at me and a dimple appeared on his left cheek. I wondered why Emily hadn't introduced me to this guy earlier.

"So, the Ethan Becker murder, huh?" He said.

I nodded. "You heard. I guess news travels."

"The detective on that case isn't pleased, Tiff. You're not going to turn into one of those PI's we hate, are you?" Emily asked.

Nick was smiling at me and I said, "I don't *want* you guys to hate me."

Emily murmured something about catching up on paperwork and disappeared and Nick asked me how long I'd been a PI. I told him it hadn't been long, and asked him how Las Vegas compared to Miami.

It was surprisingly easy to chat with him and after a few minutes, he said, "So, the guy you came in with, is he a friend or something?"

I smiled, hoping he was jealous. "No, he's just – we had to work together. Do you know him? He seems to be friends with Detective Costaki."

"'Friends' is probably an overstatement. We know him. He works in security and calls us sometimes. Has all kinds of contacts."

"That's not necessarily a bad thing."

"No. But it's worrying. His contacts aren't necessarily the kind of people you'd want to meet in a dark alley. Plus, the guy has no record."

"So he's never been arrested? Isn't that a good thing?"

Nick shook his head. "No, his record was wiped clean."

A chill went through my bones. "What does that mean?"

Nick shrugged. "It could mean a number of things. Either someone at the top really likes him, or he knows people on the inside."

I nodded and we stood in silence for a few seconds, thinking about Stone.

I figured Stone was probably out by now. "I should get going."

"Mind if I call you sometime?"

I smiled. No, I wouldn't mind.

CHAPTER TWENTY-ONE

The ride back to the Tremonte Casino was quiet. Stone was his usual non-communicative self, which was fine because I didn't feel much like talking.

This was my first case. I'd met a cute guy and I'd just discovered a murderer. Why didn't I feel happier? Sure, I was incredibly relieved to not be lying dead on the side of the road. But I was also feeling uneasy – the feeling that I'd missed something just wouldn't go away.

"Do you think she did it?" I finally asked Stone.

Stone glanced at me for a split second before focusing on the road again. I was expecting a mono-syllabic reply, so I was a bit surprised when he actually said more than two words at once. "She just told you she did."

"Yeah, she did." I'd been thinking about that. There was something strange about the way she claimed to not know Audrey, but the way she'd told me about Ethan's death, and of course the fact that she wanted to kill me after the confession, led me to believe that she was telling the truth. "But if she was going to tell me about one murder, why not talk about the other one, too? Why didn't she admit to killing Audrey as well?"

Stone shook his head. "Maybe that really was just a burglary gone bad."

"Do you think so?"

"Do you?"

I gulped, remembering the way the man in black had been waiting for me in my bedroom. He'd clean picked the lock and he was so very careful as he lay in wait. "I don't think Audrey's murder was an accident. But if Vanessa had done it, she would've told me. She was in a confessing mood."

Stone didn't say anything for a long time. And then, as we pulled up to the Tremonte, he turned to me and said, "You did really well. I'm not just saying that 'cause it's your first case. You did better than a lot of pros. Hell, you did better than the police."

That was the longest speech I'd ever heard him make and I stared at him in shock. The words only made sense after the shock had dissipated.

"Thank you," I said, unable to keep the surprise out of my voice.

Stone didn't smile, but his eyes looked happier. He nodded in the direction of the casino, wordlessly telling me to get the hell out of his car.

I smiled. "And thanks for the ride, too."

I hopped out and headed toward the parking lot. I didn't look back, but I could hear Stone drive off.

I made the drive to Sophia's place in record time. It was nice to be driving my own car again and I blasted the radio happily.

Sophia seemed a bit surprised to see me. She walked me into the living room and didn't bother with any small talk.

"What's the news?" she said.

I peered at her carefully. Her skin was pale, her hair seemed dry and limp and she'd lost weight. "Are you feeling sick?" I asked, but she shook her head.

"It's just stress. I have some bad days."

I could imagine. "I have good news," I said, "Vanessa Conigliani told me she killed Ethan. She's at the police station right now, signing a confession."

Sophia sat frozen for a few seconds, and then her whole body went limp. I saw the tears well up in her eyes and she blinked them back. "You're not kidding are you? This isn't a joke?"

"No, of course not."

I went over and wrapped my arms around her shoulders. She hugged me back and I heard her sniff.

"I'm sorry," she said, pulling away and laughing. "This has been the most incredible day. I woke up feeling sure I was going to be convicted and now this."

She laughed again and wiped away a tear. "You must think I'm crazy."

I smiled at her. "I do. But at least you're not a murderer."

Sophia began to laugh again and for a moment I worried that she'd become hysterical. But she calmed down after a minute, and managed to say, "I'll call my lawyer. I can't wait to get this ankle bracelet off!" And then she laughed madly again.

At some point, she did manage to calm down enough to call Richard Small and while we waited for him to arrive, she drove me over to a local bakery and ordered me a dozen chocolate cupcakes with chocolate icing and sprinkles.

I headed home happily with the box of cupcakes in the seat next to me. Richard and Sophia were off to the courthouse to sort out some legal stuff, I'd solved my first real case, and I had two days' worth of cupcakes sitting right beside me.

However, the feeling that I was overlooking something refused to go away.

CHAPTER TWENTY-TWO

I ate two cupcakes to celebrate, and once I was satiated with enough sugar, I decided to keep working at my night job until I had enough money saved up to quit for good. I knew I should call my parents and tell them the good news, that I had just solved my first case and was officially looking forward to a career as a private instigator. But calling my parents would also mean having to clear up that little misunderstanding about me moving in with Stone, and that was not a misunderstanding I looked forward to clearing up. Plus, before I could get the point across that Stone and I were definitely not living together, I'd probably have to listen to Nanna telling me that crotchless panties were going to be my best friend. Ugh.

I ignored the guilt I felt about shunning familial obligations, and typed up my report for Sophia until it was time to head to the Treasury Casino and pretend to be a fun-loving dealer.

It was a busy night and I worked at the roulette wheel, the craps table and then the blackjack table. Despite how busy the pit was, my thoughts kept straying to Audrey and the goons who had been threatening me. I couldn't believe that Vanessa was involved in everything, but I couldn't come up with any other explanation.

I was mindlessly dealing cards to a group of young men playing blackjack, when I noticed my pit boss hovering around. I instantly stood up straighter. Something was wrong, or else he wouldn't be hanging around near me for so long. At first I wondered if I was doing something wrong, whether I was making wrong payouts or maybe standing when I should hit. But then I noticed it was the players.

The man on the far right, a skinny, pimply fellow, had been playing at this table for quite some time. The man sitting in the middle had just joined a few hands ago. He wore glasses and had a strange, thick mustache, which I guessed was fake. Glasses was drinking a Diet Coke and Pimples sipped at a club soda. The man sitting on the far left had been nursing one whiskey for a long time.

Pimples wasn't playing much – just betting the minimum hand each time and playing right by the book. In contrast, Glasses was playing erratically. He would bet the minimum one hand and then bet wildly on the next. He lost a few small bets and once in a while he'd lose a big bet. But he was up overall, which was rare for anyone who looked and played so amateurishly.

My spidey sense was tingly and within minutes I knew that Glasses was a card counter. It was obvious to me and it was obvious to the pit boss, so I wasn't surprised when, a while later, a security guy named Mike came over and laid a hand on Glasses' shoulder.

"I think it's time for you to leave," Mike said quietly, and Glasses didn't bother to argue. He collected his chips and left.

"You too," Mike said to Pimples, who nodded and made a beeline for the exit.

Mike vanished as unobtrusively as he'd appeared, and the drunk guy on the left ordered another whiskey.

"Hey," he said to me. "Card-counters, huh? I guess they were in on it together."

I made a non-committal noise and kept dealing. A couple of young women came to the table and joined him and as I dealt, I noticed that Whiskey Guy was actually a pretty good player. He was winning fairly regularly and after a few more hands, he got up, gave me a wink, and left.

And then it hit me. Whiskey Guy was a pretty good card counter. More importantly, he knew how to stay under the radar. And that's how Audrey's murder had happened.

I spent the rest of the night in a haze, wondering how I'd failed to see it before. I'm still not sure how I restrained myself from making the phone call right then, but somehow I managed to get to sleep without waking anyone at an ungodly hour.

The next morning, the first thing I did was to call Neil Durant. "How's it going?" I asked. "Have you looked into Steven's scam?"

He sounded glum. "Yes. You were right."

"Well?"

"It's too soon to prove, but we're collecting evidence. The guy's got a massive ring of dealers working for him and security guys covering his tracks." He was silent for a moment and then said hopefully, "You wouldn't consider working with us on this, would you? You know, photograph his meetings and stuff. Maybe even pretend to be a dealer?"

I smiled wryly. My first offer to work in casino security and I'd have to turn it down. "I'm sorry. Steven already knows who I am. And he's got some thugs sicced on me, so I better stay out of his way."

"Oh." Neil was silent for a moment. "Congrats on getting Vanessa, by the way."

"Thanks." I had a brilliant idea and said, "Would you tell Steven that we caught the guy? Or girl, in this case. Maybe then he'll call off his guys."

"Yeah. Sorry I couldn't be more help."

"That's cool," I said, and we hung up.

My next call was to Max Desilva. He sounded as mellow as ever.

"Max," I said urgently, "When you were stalking Steven, did you ever see him go out on a date?"

"Sure," he said, "I saw him once or twice in a fancy restaurant with this woman."

"Did you get her name?"

"No, 'fraid not."

"What did she look like?"

196

"Um, let me think. Brunette hair, slightly chubby. In her twenties, I'd say."

"Great! You've been an incredible help!"

That was all I needed, and as I said goodbye, I warned him that he might be asked to testify about the woman he saw.

"That's fine," he said, his good mood undiminished.

My next call was to Emily.

"Hey Tiffany," she answered, "Didn't I tell you you'd like Nick?"

I laughed. "Yeah. Thanks for introducing us. But that's not why I'm calling."

"Oh?"

"Who's the detective dealing with Audrey's murder?"

"Detective Martinez *was*. That case's closed."

"Not anymore. Tell Martinez to check the fingerprints he found at Audrey's place with fingerprints of this guy. Steven Macarthur. He's being investigated by the Riverbelle for casino fraud and he's got a bunch of thugs working for him. If his prints don't match up, one of his thugs' might."

There was silence for a moment, and then Emily said, "What makes you so sure?"

"I have my reasons."

"Let me hear them."

I sighed. "Fine, it's like this. I thought Ethan and Audrey's murders were connected. But I realized last night that they didn't have to be connected – it could just be one person taking advantage of existing conditions. Like the fact that Ethan was already dead."

"That doesn't implicate Steven Macarthur in any way."

"Ok. But Audrey was dating a big shot at the Riverbelle casino. Everyone knew that. We all thought it was Ethan, but turns out it wasn't. It wasn't Neil either. The only other big shot left is the manager, Steven. And Steven was seen dating a girl matching Audrey's description –"

"By who?'

"Um, does it matter?"

"It does, actually."

"Fine. By the ex-manager of the Riverbelle. He knew Steven well." I left out the part that he had also been stalking Steven. "Anyway, Audrey discovered the scam. I'm not sure if she discovered it on her own or if Steven told her, but after she found out, she was considering telling Ethan. Steven managed to keep her quiet for a while by bribing her with expensive jewelry, but then she realized she was making a mistake and snapped."

"And then Ethan was killed."

"Exactly. Steven wouldn't have hurt Ethan himself – if his scam came to light, he would've just convinced Ethan that he had been framed or something, and would have gotten away with it. But nobody else adored him the way Ethan did, so he couldn't risk anyone else finding out. He convinced the board to can the audit, but Audrey was still threatening to tell Neil. So he threatened Audrey, and when that didn't work, he wound up killing her. It was him or someone he hired."

Emily was silent for a pretty long time. Finally, she said, "That's an interesting theory and I'll pass it on to Martinez. Let's see if it holds up."

"Thanks," I said. "I hope the Ethan Becker case wasn't just beginner's luck."

I could just about hear Emily shaking her head. "You're a good PI, Tiff. I'm sure beginner's luck has nothing to do with your work."

CHAPTER TWENTY-THREE

I tried to spread the word at the Riverbelle that I'd finished with my investigating. But I wasn't too sure how well the news had spread, so just to be on the safe side, I was staying at the Tremonte for a few more days. Just till Steven was arrested and put behind bars. Detective Martinez had assured me that it would happen sooner rather than later – Steven's fingerprints had matched those found in Audrey's apartment, and waiters at the restaurant had corroborated Max's story about Steven and Audrey being seen on a romantic date.

I'd visited Glen one day and told him where I was staying, so for the past few days Glen had been coming over to the hotel in the morning and enjoying their buffet breakfasts with me. He didn't have as large an appetite as I did, but we both enjoyed the free food, and I admitted to him that I was a PI, and the man chasing me hadn't been my boyfriend. The news didn't faze him one bit, and he promised that as soon as I moved back into my condo I was welcome to come over for cupcakes whenever I wanted.

A few days ago, I'd gone over to my parents' for lunch. When I turned up alone on the doorstep, my mom and Nanna looked at me glumly.

"You broke up already?" Mom said. "I knew I should've bought you some nice clothes to wear."

"Huh," Nanna said. "And I knew I should've gone to Victoria's Secret with you. You know they've got these nice thong panties now?"

I glared at both of them. "We were never together. I never moved in with him. You just misheard me."

They seemed to not have heard the bit about me and Stone not being a couple.

My mom smiled. "You never moved in with him? Well, I guess that's a relief."

"Yup." Nanna nodded. "I don't care what they say about these modern times. You move in with a man, he's never gonna marry you. You remember that now."

I sighed.

Nanna went on. "You gotta go to Victoria's Secret though, I know you're still wearing your high school cotton undies. No wonder you can't get a man. I'll bet Stone likes the new, silky stuff they've got in stores these days."

I glared at both of them and walked into the den where Dad was watching CNN.

"Where's Stone?" he asked, looking mildly surprised.

"He's not here," Nanna declared from behind me. "Tiffany's going to play it slow."

Dad nodded. "That's good. I don't want you moving with a man we barely know."

I gave him a hug and said, "I wouldn't move in with someone without telling you. But, I do have big news!"

Nanna gasped. "You're pregnant! And the baby's not Stone's!"

I glared at her. "How would that even happen?"

She shrugged and looked bored. "That's what they always say in soap operas."

Mom looked at me carefully. "She's not pregnant," she told Nanna, and then turned back to me. "You're not, are you?"

I shook my head. "No. But I am a private investigator!"

I told them about how I'd worked for Sophia and solved the Ethan Becker murder *and* who was behind Audrey's death. At the end of it, Dad said, "You should be careful, hon."

I looked at him and smiled. I'd left out the parts about scary thugs and people breaking into my condo, but Dad still looked concerned.

"I am careful," I said, "I'm taking Krav Maga classes and I just got a gun permit."

Mom gasped and made disapproving noises about using firearms.

Nanna said, "I knew about it all along! Didn't I, Tiff?" She turned to Mom triumphantly. "See, she tells me stuff. So if she *was* pregnant, she would've told me before she told you."

Mom looked at me. "You'd tell me if you were pregnant, wouldn't you?"

I almost threw up my hands in despair. "Of course I would. But I'm not. I don't even have a boyfriend."

"Except for Stone," said my mom. "You be nice to him, I can tell he likes you."

Nanna said, "What's Krav Maga? Sounds pretty trendy. Maybe I should take classes with you."

I promised Nanna I'd take her with me to Krav Maga one day, and Mom began quizzing me about Stone and my non-existent love-life. No matter how much I tried to explain that Stone and I were just friends, Nanna insisted on giving me advice about flirting with other men to make him jealous, and Mom gave me a recipe for chicken casserole that was 'sure to win a real man's heart.'

I suffered through it all, because that's what good daughters do. And then I went home, with a belly full of yummy home cooking, and a doggie bag full of leftovers.

I met Stone at eleven in the morning and he drove toward North Las Vegas. Since I was living in the Tremonte, I no longer needed his protection and it was the first time I'd seen him in a while. The ride was as wordless, as usual. I felt like I should say something, maybe thank him for his help. But I didn't. I just switched on the radio to fill up the silence and changed the station to one that played the latest hits. Immediately, Stone switched it back to a country music station and I looked at him in surprise.

"Really?" I said. "The dog died and the wife ran off and you're singing the blues? I didn't take you for that kind of guy."

"What kind of guy did you take me to be?"

The question threw me. I'd taken him to be the kind of guy who... No, I drew a blank.

We got out at the gun shop and Stone helped me select my very first gun, a Smith & Wesson. I knew I'd be uncomfortable carrying it, let alone using it, for a long time - until I had enough practice - and Stone seemed to read my mind. He drove us to a nearby gun range and we shot at paper targets in silence.

After a couple of rounds, Stone took off his protective earmuffs and came over to talk to me.

"How's it going at the Tremonte?"

I was surprised he was actually making conversation, but I think I did a good job of not raising my eyebrows into my hairline.

"It's ok," I said. "I think I'll stay on until Steven's finally behind bars."

He nodded. "Wise choice. Hope Sophia's paying for it."

I smiled. "Yeah, she is."

"Great job on your case. You didn't need to keep chasing Audrey's killer after you'd nabbed Ethan's."

"Thanks," I said, a bit surprised by the praise.

"But," he said, "You need to work on your Krav Maga. Carla tells me you're not hitting hard enough when you punch the groin."

We grinned at each other and I was about to go back to firing practice when Stone said, "I think you'd fit in well at Stonehedge Security, if you're ever interested in doing some work for us. Of course, you'd have to get better at hitting people before that."

I smiled at him. "I'll keep that in mind."

"Are you dating Nick Carlton?"

The question came out of the blue and I looked at him in surprise. "What makes you think I am?"

He shrugged. "Little clues."

"Do you know him?"

"No. But I guess he knows of me."

"Yeah. He did warn me about you."

Stone raised one eyebrow. "And are you warned?"

"I'm not sure," I said, smiling. "Should I be?"

Stone smiled back and didn't reply. He walked back to his side of the shooting range and put his earmuffs back on.

I watched him for a few seconds, the way he shot his targets, the way his hair fell slightly over his forehead and the way he could wrap you in a quiet blanket of security.

And then I went back to practicing my shots.

If you enjoyed this first book in the Tiffany Black humorous mystery series, make sure you check out book two, SECRETS IN LAS VEGAS, which will be available in November.

Excerpt from SECRETS IN LAS VEGAS

I was walking down the street, minding my own business, when the man fell out of the sky.

It was the noise – a loud, rustling sound like the wings of a great bird - that made me turn and look at him. I was just in time to see him crouch down and land neatly on his feet. His stance was elegant, cat-like and poised, and his noisy parachute drifted down gently behind him. He stood up straight, unclipped the parachute hooks and bundled it under his arm.

I stared at him in shock. I've seen a lot of crazy things, living and working in Vegas, but I'd never seen anything quite like this.

He was tall, a hair over six feet, and wore an impeccably tailored suit, black gloves, and a black ski-mask that hid his face, leaving only his eyes visibly. Despite the ski-mask, he didn't seem dangerous in the least, and I found myself wondering where he'd fallen from. Skyscrapers rose up on both sides of this deserted off-Strip side-street, and he could've jumped out of any one of them. Once he'd gotten the parachute under control, he noticed me staring at him.

When our eyes met I felt the air leave my body in a sudden whoosh. He had the most intense, deep green eyes I'd ever seen, and I felt a strange shiver run up my spine.

His eyes smiled at me, and then he winked, turned around and stepped into a nearby parked Ferrari.

The car sped off within seconds, and I was left standing there, wondering just what the hell had happened.

ABOUT THE AUTHOR

A.R. Winters loves books, TV series and movies about mysteries, crime capers and heists. She also enjoys a good laugh, so she writes lighthearted, humorous mysteries.

She lives with her husband in mercurial Melbourne, Australia. When not writing, she's usually eating too much cake.

Connect with her online:
http://twitter.com/ar_winters
http://www.arwinters.com

JOIN THE A.R. WINTERS NEWSLETTER! WIN $100!

Beginning in November, I'll be giving away a $100 gift card* on the 1st of the month, and every month after, to one newsletter subscriber. The winner will be announced inside the newsletter; you'll have to actually open it to see who won :-) In addition to the chance to win $100, newsletter subscribers also get exclusive discounts on A.R. Winters' upcoming novels.

*Deliverable online. Contest open to all subscribers including international readers.

Join at www.arwinters.com/newsletter

If you enjoyed reading Innocent in Las Vegas, I would appreciate it if you would help others enjoy this book, too.

Lend it. This book is lending-enabled, so please, share it with a friend.

Recommend it. Please help other readers find this book by recommending it to friends, readers' groups and discussion boards.

Review it. Please tell other readers why you liked this book by reviewing it at Amazon or Goodreads. If you do write a review, please send me an email at arwintersfiction@gmail.com so I can thank you personally, or visit me at http://www.arwinters.com

Made in the USA
San Bernardino, CA
17 April 2018